"You have a hankering for my DNA?"

Nick paused, undecipherable emotion in his eyes. "You're serious."

More than Sage wanted to admit. She'd been trying to work up the nerve to approach him since the first time they'd hit the sheets. And it was no wonder. It wasn't just his mesmerizing sky blue eyes, thick, dark hair or masculine good looks. But intelligence and kindness, practicality and innovation, compassion and heart...

And that something special that was all his own. But she couldn't tell him that. Not without sounding like she'd really gone round the bend.

"You are everything I'd ever want in a baby daddy."

His sexy grin encouraged her to go on.

"Big. Strong. Handsome."

He tilted his head, edges of his lips curving seductively. "And here I thought you liked me for my brain."

"I do." She batted her lashes flirtatiously. "Your sense of humor, too."

He grinned. "We do know how to make each other laugh."

Which was the way they both liked it. Nice. Easy. Uncomplicated.

This could be, too. If only she could make him see...

Dear Reader,

We've all done it. Made detailed plans, only to see them go hopelessly awry. We've also done the opposite. Made a grand plan with absolutely no details, intending to get by on the fly. Only to have that implode, too. So where is the happy medium?

Sage Lockhart's romantic dreams have fallen apart. She still wants to have a child. But this time she is not taking any chances. She's going into the situation with a clear-eyed vision and a proposal.

Nick Monroe has always pushed hard and fast for what he wants. That hasn't worked out for him, either. Now he's trying to learn to be patient. To accept what can be given to him, without ruining everything by ambitiously wanting more.

So when Nick and Sage decide to have a child together, they set boundaries. No pressure, no expectations and definitely no romance! They will remain lovers and friends, take each day as it comes and share the baby they are now happily expecting. Until marriage becomes unexpectedly necessary. Then all bets are off. And both are forced to figure out exactly what they want all over again...

For information on other books in this series, and so much more, please visit me at cathygillenthacker.com.

Happy reading!

Cathy Gillen Thacker

WANTED:
TEXAS DADDY

—

CATHY GILLEN THACKER

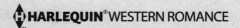

Recycling programs
for this product may
not exist in your area.

ISBN-13: 978-0-373-75761-9

Wanted: Texas Daddy

Copyright © 2017 by Cathy Gillen Thacker

Printed in U.S.A.

www.Harlequin.com

Cathy Gillen Thacker is married and a mother of three. She and her husband spent eighteen years in Texas and now reside in North Carolina. Her mysteries, romantic comedies and heartwarming family stories have made numerous appearances on bestseller lists, but her best reward, she says, is knowing one of her books made someone's day a little brighter. A popular Harlequin author for many years, she loves telling passionate stories with happy endings and thinks nothing beats a good romance and a hot cup of tea! You can visit Cathy's website, cathygillenthacker.com, for more information on her upcoming and previously published books, recipes and a list of her favorite things.

Books by Cathy Gillen Thacker

Harlequin Western Romance

Texas Legacies: The Lockharts

A Texas Soldier's Family
A Texas Cowboy's Christmas
The Texas Valentine Twins

Harlequin American Romance

McCabe Homecoming

The Texas Lawman's Woman
The Long, Hot Texas Summer
The Texas Christmas Gift
The Texas Wildcatter's Baby

Legends of Laramie County

The Reluctant Texas Rancher
The Texas Rancher's Vow
The Texas Rancher's Marriage
The Texas Rancher's Family

Visit the Author Profile page
at Harlequin.com for more titles.

Chapter One

"You want to have my baby," Nick Monroe repeated slowly, leading the two horses out of the stables.

Sage Lockhart slid a booted foot into the stirrup and swung herself up into the saddle. She'd figured the Monroe Ranch was the perfect place to have this discussion. Not only was it Nick's ancestral home, but with Nick the only one living there now, it was completely private.

She drew her flat-brimmed hat straight across her brow. "An unexpected request, I know."

Yet, she realized as she studied him, noting that the color of his eyes was the same deep blue as the big Texas sky above, he didn't look all that shocked.

For he better than anyone knew how much she wanted a child. They'd grown quite close ever since she returned to Texas, to claim her inheritance from her late father and help her mother weather a scandal that had rocked the Lockhart family to the core.

So close, in fact, the two of them had been "friends with benefits" for several months now.

Nick's gaze drifted over her, creating small wildfires in its wake.

With a click of his reins, he turned his horse in the direction of the wide-open pastures behind the Triple Canyon ranch house. He slowed his mount slightly, while waiting for Sage to catch up. "You're still having second thoughts about using an anonymous donor from the fertility clinic?"

She nodded, enjoying the warm autumn breeze blowing over them. It was a perfect Indian summer afternoon.

Swallowing around the knot of emotion in her throat, Sage admitted, "On the one hand, picking out a potential daddy for my baby via a set of statistics and characteristics seems easy enough."

Squinting at her, he settled his hat on his head. "Kind of like reading a menu of options."

"Right." If only it were that simple, she thought wistfully. Because her mom had been right. Having a baby was an emotional—not a scientific—proposition.

"But?" He kept the pace slow and steady as they threaded their way along a path that took them down a steep ravine, across a wildflower-strewn canyon and up the other side.

"It's a lot more complicated than I thought it would be." Mostly, because the only person she could see fathering her baby was the ruggedly handsome rancher-businessman beside her.

She drew a deep, bolstering breath. "The idea of a complete stranger fathering my child is becoming increasingly unappealing." When they reached their favorite picnic spot, she swung herself out of the saddle, watching as Nick tied their horses to a tree.

Together, they moved into the warm early September sunshine. Spread a blanket out on the ground. "What if the donor profiles aren't exactly accurate?"

Nick set down the rucksack containing their meal. "I thought the clinic had everyone go through extensive background checks."

Sage settled cross-legged on the blanket. watching as he did the same. "They do."

He opened up the bag, brought out the containers from her café-bistro. Two individual thermoses of chicken tortilla soup. Luscious squares of jalapeño-cheese cornbread. And for dessert, triple-berry tarts that she'd gotten up at the crack of dawn to make especially for him.

"Then…?"

Sage shrugged. Aware that Nick was carefully weighing his options—the way he always did when the talk turned to anything personal—Sage forced herself to abandon the hopelessly idyllic notions that had dictated her actions for years, and speak what was on her mind, rather than what was in her heart.

"The more I think about it, the more I have to wonder. Do I *really* want some stranger's DNA swimming around inside me?"

Nick grinned, as if pleased to hear she was a one-man woman, at least in this respect.

He looked at her from beneath the brim of his hat. "Which is why you're asking me?" he countered in the rough, sexy tone she'd fallen in love with the first second she had heard it. "Because you know me?"

Sage locked eyes with him, not sure whether he was teasing her or not. One thing she knew for sure: there hadn't been a time since they'd first met that she *hadn't* wanted him.

And that, too, was unusual. Prior to meeting Nick, she hadn't considered herself a particularly sexual person.

He'd changed all that. Fast. Thanks to the times they'd spent in bed, she now knew how much she loved the physical side of affection.

Even *without* the heretofore requisite falling in love.

"Or because," he continued flirtatiously as he unscrewed the lid on his thermos, "you have a hankering for my DNA?"

Aware the only appetite she had now was not for food, she quipped, "How about both?"

He paused, spoon halfway to his lips, undecipherable emotion in his eyes. "You're serious."

More than she wanted to admit. She'd been trying to work up the nerve to approach him since the first time they'd hit the sheets. And it was no wonder she felt he was the perfect man for the job. It wasn't just his mesmerizing sky blue eyes, thick, dark hair or masculine good looks. Or the way he made her feel in bed, all woman to his man. At six foot four inches tall, with broad shoulders and a fit, muscular body, he was the quintessential Texas cowboy. A man who was as much at ease running his family's business as he was this ranch. He radiated not just boundless energy and good health, but intelligence and kindness, practicality and innovation, compassion and heart...

But she couldn't tell him any of that. Not without sounding like she'd really gone round the bend. "Well..." With a wistful sigh, she flashed him a teasing look. "You are everything I'd ever want in a baby daddy."

His sexy grin encouraged her to go on.

"Big. Strong. Handsome."

He tilted his head, edges of his lips curving seductively. "And here I thought you liked me for my brain."

"I do." She batted her lashes flirtatiously. "Your sense of humor, too."

He grinned. "We do know how to make each other laugh."

Which was the way they both liked it. Nice. Easy. Uncomplicated. This could be, too. If only she could make him see so...

She covered his big hand with her own. Gave it a squeeze. "And since we're already friends, with benefits, conceiving wouldn't require us to do anything we're not already doing. Except," she added, unable to prevent a self-conscious flush, "forgetting to use protection."

Clearing his throat, he looked her in the eye. "Nice as that sounds..."

Her heart took on a rapid, uneven beat.

Fearing rejection, she persuaded swiftly, "You want kids, too." She removed her hand from his, sat back. "You've said so, at least half a dozen times."

He nodded, his beautiful mouth set in a sober line. "When the time is right. Yeah, Sage, I do."

Restless, she leaped to her feet. Hands knotted at her sides, she began to pace. "What if it's never right?" She whirled back to face him then watched as he rose, too. "What if, like me—" her tone grew as strangled as the hopes inside her "—you don't find someone and fall madly in love? What if we wait too long and then something happens and we find we're no longer as fertile as we once were and we suddenly *can't* have children? I don't want to live with that kind of regret, Nick. Especially since I've already wasted so much time."

"Chasing after Timothy Wellington."

"Terrence Whittier," she corrected, aware that was the one thing he could never get right, her ex's name. "And you're right, I don't want to do that again. Live so far in the future that I don't appreciate the here and now. I don't want that for you, either, Nick." She trod closer, hands raised beseechingly. "And since..."

She stopped, aware in her eagerness to convince him, she may have spoken a bit too bluntly.

"I've already had two broken engagements?"

Knowing she had no room to talk, given her own relationship failure, she wrapped her hand around his bicep. Felt it swell beneath her touch.

"My point is," she continued, her fingers curving intimately around the hard-packed muscle, through the soft chambray of his shirt, "you've been no more successful at finding the perfect match than I have." She stepped back, jerked in a breath, gave it one last shot. "So why not accept that the odds are against us? And simply make it happen, on our own terms."

SAGE HAD A POINT, Nick knew.

Waiting might bring them everything they wanted. The kind of fantastic, enduring love he knew Sage still dreamed about—even if she wouldn't admit it. And it might bring them nothing. Hadn't he put off pursuing his long-held dreams for too long? An orphan since age ten, he knew better than anyone how short life could be. Still, there were problems with her proposition. The least of which were his growing feelings for her. Compared with the way she still felt—might always feel—about him. As a friend. A bed buddy. Nothing more.

And although their casual arrangement was fine for now—more than fine actually, since he had so much else going on, work-wise—he wasn't sure that would always be the case.

Because like most deeply ambitious souls, he knew this about himself. He always wanted more.

And that was never more true than when it came to Sage Lockhart. She was five feet nine inches of nonstop energy and enthusiasm, her slender body as feminine as it was curvaceous. With a breathtakingly beautiful face, mesmerizing golden-brown eyes, soft pink bow-shaped lips and a thick mane of wheat-colored hair that fell in soft waves to her shoulders, she drove him wild with lust. It didn't matter if she was dressed in fancy cowgirl attire, like she sported now, or the white chef's coat she wore to work, he was constantly wanting to pull her into his arms and make love to her.

Unfortunately, making her physically his wouldn't solve this dilemma.

Sobering, Nick put on the brakes. "As much as I want a family of my own, too, you know I'm married to the Monroe family business right now."

As always, at the first hint of conflict, a wall went up. "That's just it, Nick. I'm not asking that marriage be part of this equation. Not now. Not ever."

"Even when you become pregnant and/or the baby is born."

"Even then."

She said that, but did she actually mean it? Nick studied Sage skeptically. "Yet, to hear your family talk, you're one of the most hopelessly romantic women ever born."

"I used to be. Before I met you."

Ouch.

She waved an airy hand. "You made me realize that reality is better than romance any day," she confided in a sweet, matter-of-fact voice.

He tamped down his disappointment. Faced her with his legs braced apart, arms folded in front of him. "How so?"

"You and I started out as just friends."

Only, he thought, because she would have refused to date him in the tumult of the family scandal that had brought her back to Texas in early June. Then, she had wanted to concentrate on helping her shell-shocked mother clear the Lockhart name of any wrongdoing, while also figuring out what to do with her own inheritance from her late father—a commercial building, complete with a personal residence, on Laramie, Texas's historic Main Street.

Over the course of the summer, Sage had accomplished both, while her "friendship" with him had morphed into a no-strings-attached affair.

She had opened a thriving café-bistro, The Cowgirl Chef, which was just down the street from his own family venue, Monroe's Western Wear. She'd also moved off her mother's Circle H Ranch and into the apartment above her coffee shop.

"And because we got to know each other platonically first before we fell into bed, we never viewed each other through rose-colored glasses." She stepped close enough he caught the intoxicating scent of her perfume. "The point is, Nick, we were honest with each other. About everything from Day One."

Except for one thing, he thought.

How much I wanted to be with you.

Sage might have *fallen* into a sexual relationship with him, but he had known all along that he wanted to make her his woman. Luckily, she had felt the chemistry between them, too. Sighing, she looked up at him from beneath her lashes and went on, "I've never had to pretend to want things I didn't want, just to be with you. The way I did with Terrence."

Instead, he realized ironically, it was him, pretending he didn't want the things he did. Not that this current roadblock was going to stop him. He would win her heart, no matter how long it took.

"Like marriage," he guessed, keeping his attitude as ultracasual as hers.

The soft swell of her breasts rose and fell. "It's not for me." She gripped his forearms beseechingly. "And since you're as wedded to your family business as I am to my new café-bistro, we make a perfect pair."

That much he could agree on. He'd never met a woman who fascinated him the way Sage did.

That being the case, maybe he should be a gentleman, try it her way. "So how would this work?" he asked curiously. If there was anything his own joke-of-a-love-life had taught him, it was never to crowd a woman. Never jump the gun. It was slow and steady patience that would win out in the end. A tact that had moved them from friends, to lovers and possibly parents, thus far. He took her all the way into his arms. "Us having a baby together?"

Sage splayed her hands across his chest. "As you might imagine…"

Oh, he could imagine, all right, he thought, body already hardening.

"…first, we get me pregnant," she teased, her golden-brown eyes gleaming with excitement.

Nick savored the feel of her soft body pressed up against his. "Can't say I mind working on that part…" he admitted huskily, kissing her temple. It would give him ample opportunity to make love with her again and again.

And every time he made love to her, he felt her stubborn resistance to real, enduring commitment slip, just a little bit.

Sage shrugged. "Then we have the baby and parent him or her together."

"Under one roof?"

She stepped back, clamping her arms in front of her. "Well, I don't think we have to go that far…"

What if I want to go that far?

She lifted her hand before he could interject. "I think it would be smart to maintain separate residences. You can live at your family ranch, I'll keep my apartment in town. And we can care for the baby at both places. Be together as much or as little as we want."

That sounded okay, since he knew better than anyone how one thing could easily lead to another, with Sage.

Soberly, he warned, "You know, if my quest for venture capital comes through, and I can expand into half a dozen new stores in different locations the way I'd like, I'll be traveling some."

Sage smiled, unperturbed. "That's the beauty of my being here in Laramie. I have my whole family, you have yours. Between the Monroes and the Lockharts, we'll have more backup with this baby than we know what to do with whether you're in town or not."

That was true.

Was it possible they could both have everything they wanted?

Especially since marriage per se didn't mean all that much to him, either. What he really wanted was to be with Sage. Having a baby with her, well…that was the stuff of dreams, too.

"Sounds like you've got it all figured out," he drawled.

"We can have it all, Nick. Friendship. Sex. Family. Plus, the freedom to live our lives exactly as we want and pursue our careers without constraint." She toyed with the top button of his shirt. "So what do you say?"

The only thing he could if he wanted to make Sage his. He lowered his head and took possession of her lips. "Darlin'?" He kissed her again, more tenderly and persuasively now. "Consider me 'all in'…"

Chapter Two

Four months later

Nick put the closed sign on the door of Monroe's Western Wear and turned back to Sage.

Wheat-gold hair swept up into an untidy knot on the back of her head, her face glowing with the unmistakable light of happiness and maternal good health, she looked more gorgeous than he had ever seen her.

But the time for avoiding this conversation was over.

He walked through the rustic interior of the store, his attitude as stern as hers was stubborn. "Enough of this evading, Sage. We have to tell people." The sooner the better, as far as he was concerned.

Sage ducked her head to avoid meeting his gaze, and continued sorting through the stack of women's jeans. "In a couple of weeks," she murmured, zeroing in on another size up from her normal.

He resisted the urge to direct her over to the small but well-outfitted area containing denim maternity wear. Settling with his back against the heavy wood display rack, so she would have no choice but to look at him, he asked, "You really think you can keep hiding this?"

Her lower lip thrust out into a kissable pout. "The chef's coat and colorful aprons have worked so far."

Actually, Nick thought, his gaze sliding down her newly voluptuous body, they hadn't. It wasn't just the waist and hips of the garment that were snug—the double row of buttons over her newly luscious breasts were so tight, they threatened to pop off.

Deciding, however, that might not be the best thing for him to point out, he merely inclined his head. "Your family has been giving me looks."

"So?" She shrugged again. "They give everyone they think has designs on me looks."

Not, he thought, the kind of looks they'd been giving *him*. He cleared his throat, regarded her severely, tried again. "Sage..."

She started to dart past him, then stopped, spying a Bullhaven Ranch pickup truck parking in one of the slanted spaces in front of the store. Her pretty mouth dropped into an O of surprise.

"Oh, heck!" she swore, darting off in the opposite direction toward the back of the store. "There's Chance!" She ducked through the curtain that led to the storeroom, calling over her shoulder. "If he asks, I'm not here!"

Well, this ought to be fun, Nick thought wryly, as a second, then third pickup pulled up next to the first. Three tall men emerged from the driver's seats. Headed toward the front of the store.

Chance Lockhart peered around the closed sign. Gestured. He wanted in. So did his two brothers.

Figuring they may as well get this over with, Nick obliged. Garrett, Wyatt and Chance Lockhart stalked in. Not surprisingly, all three of Sage's older brothers looked loaded for bear. The only sibling not there was her Special Forces brother, Zane, who was as usual off on assignment. Garrett nodded perfunctorily at Nick. "Monroe."

This was not looking good. "What can I do for you?" Nick asked.

Wyatt jumped in with a suspicious glare. "For starters, tell us what in blazes is going on between you and Sage."

"Not sure what you mean."

Chance squinted. "Are the two of you a couple? Or what?"

It took everything Nick had to suppress a groan. "I imagine Sage would classify us in the 'or what' category."

Garrett's frown deepened. "Not funny, Monroe."

"Mom is worried sick," Chance added.

Lucille Lockhart was a wonderful woman. Kind and generous to a fault. Nick did not want to cause her grief.

"She needn't be." He would care for and protect Lucille's only female child with every fiber of his being.

"Really?" Wyatt demanded, slamming his hands on his waist. "Because from where we're standing, it looks as if Sage has some pretty big news to share."

So they did suspect, just as Nick had figured. Pushing aside his irritation that Sage had let it come to this, he said, "Then maybe you should be asking her."

The brothers' expressions turned even grimmer. "We have," Wyatt groused. "She won't tell us anything."

Sounded familiar.

Suddenly, he felt sympathy for her family, even as he remained boxed in by his first obligation, which was to Sage. "What do you want me to do?" he demanded impatiently. It wasn't like he could control Sage. No one could.

"Cowboy up," Chance said.

Garrett nodded. "Show some responsibility."

The intimation that he hadn't stung.

Nick thought about all the times he'd held Sage while she cried—uncharacteristically—over the silliest things. How he'd taken it in stride when she'd fallen asleep, mid-just-about-anything, and/or asked him not to touch her breasts because her nipples were just too sensitive. Surpassed what he really wanted—like sizzling fajitas or a big juicy rare steak—and instead dined on what she was having, even if it was ginger ale and crackers.

Resentment knotted his gut. "How do you know I haven't been?"

A skeptical silence fell.

Finally, Garrett said, "Have you asked her to marry you?"

Without warning, the curtain behind them was ripped aside. Sage stormed out, temper flaring.

This, too, was par for the course. Since conceiving, her emotions had frequently skyrocketed out of control.

"Whoa, Nellie!" Hormones raging, she marched toward her brothers, shooing them away with both arms. "You guys need to back the heck off!"

Her brothers remained where they were.

And suddenly, Nick knew what had to be done. Whether Sage liked it or not.

"They're right." He pivoted back toward her, wrapping an arm around her shoulders. "The time for pretending there's nothing going on with us has passed, darlin'."

Giving her no chance to protest, he swung back to her three brothers. "Sage is pregnant." He paused to let the words sink in. Aware in that moment he had never been prouder, or happier. "And the baby is mine."

"WELL, THAT WENT BADLY," Nick admitted, the moment Sage's brothers had left, more than a little disappointed to find out the two of them had no plans to marry.

"You think?" Sage paced back and forth between the aisles. She'd thought Nick was on her side in this! Fuming, she gave him a sharp look. "Now it's only a matter of time before they tell Mom I'm pregnant with your child."

His eyes lit up the way they always did when he knew he'd gotten under her skin. "First of all—" Nick shrugged, as if not sure what the big deal was "—you *are* pregnant. And your brothers are right—you can't hide it much longer. So unless you cowgirl up and have that talk with your mother—and soon—they'll be forced to spill."

As always, his ultramasculine presence, the sun-warmed leather scent of him, made her feel protected and intensely aware. In an attempt to keep her equilibrium, she kept her distance from him. "That's not really a comfort to me, Nick."

He rubbed his hand across his closely shaven jaw, then lazily dropped it again, his eyes never leaving hers. "Hey, I call it like I see it. And for the record, Sage? I'd like to tell *my* family you're carrying my baby, too!"

The bell above the door dinged.

Sage moaned, thinking it was probably her brothers, back for Round Two of Convince Sage To Do The Traditional Thing. Instead, the interloper was a gorgeous, elegantly dressed young woman Sage had never seen before.

Nick looked surprised but pleased as he moved to shake the lady's hand. "MR! What are you doing here? I thought our meeting wasn't until tomorrow."

This was the lauded MR? Sage thought in shock. From the way Nick had talked about the venture capital executive, she had imagined someone older and stodgier. Not some auburn-haired beauty sporting stylish black eyeglasses who could double as a Hollywood starlet.

Not that Nick had indicated he had noticed MR's stunning good looks.

He turned back to Sage, backtracking long enough

to make introductions. "Sage, this is MR Rhodes, from Metro Equity Partners. She's the venture capital exec I've been working with. MR, this is—"

"Your fiancée?" the exec guessed tartly.

So she was stodgy after all, considering her disapproving tone as her gaze moved knowingly to Sage's tummy.

"Ah—" For the first time since the other woman had entered the store, Nick looked flummoxed.

"Baby mama?" MR guessed again, with a candid smile that did not reach her eyes.

The set of Nick's mouth was suddenly as tense as his shoulders. "Did you want to talk business this evening?" he asked brusquely.

MR got the hint. "Briefly, I do. We're very close to getting approval from the other partners for the deal you and I have been negotiating."

A long, slow back and forth of ideas that had been going on as long as Sage had known Nick. "That's great news!" he said.

MR scowled, suddenly seeming as reluctant and unhappy as Nick had a second ago. "It would be, if you weren't in the midst of a *situation*."

Oh, dear. "Maybe I should leave," Sage said.

"No." Nick clapped a possessive hand on her shoulder. He gave her a look that said they had nothing to hide. "You stay."

Okay, then.

He turned back to MR. "What do you mean by *situation*?"

MR huffed and looked at Sage as if she were a spoiler. "The plan is to make Nick the public face of the new Western-wear stores. Have him featured prominently in every ad, with personal appearances at every location. But we can't do that if he's a deadbeat dad."

Deadbeat dad? "Nick is not shirking his responsibility," Sage said hotly.

"I know my partners. They are old-school, family men. There is no way they're going to go for the new company spokesperson—the brand representative, if you will—having a kid out of wedlock. It's just not going to happen." MR looked Nick in the eye. "So unless you want to be trapped here in this one-horse town, in this one-horse store, in perpetuity, the two of you need to get hitched. Pronto."

Sage turned to Nick in a panic. She didn't want him to lose everything he had been working so hard to achieve, any more than she wanted to be backed into a corner herself. To her relief, he reached over and gave her hand an understanding squeeze.

"What if we had the rest of my family—my three sisters and brother, and all my nephews and nieces—in the ads?" Nick proposed. "Maybe even use photos of the rest of the Monroe clan. We could go back as far as the store's beginnings, which is four generations."

"No. You are the one they want to see in all the ads. And you can see why, right?" MR turned to Sage in full business mode. "He's like a younger, hotter, tall-dark-and-handsome Ralph Lauren. Our vision and the success of the new venture hinges on Nick's sex appeal, his image as an upstanding cowboy and devoted family man. And with you pregnant, Sage, regardless of how either of you feel about it, that means marriage. ASAP."

"We can't make a decision like that on the fly," Nick countered.

"Understandable. You all need to talk about it. In the

meantime, my assistant, Everett Keller, is checking into the Laramie Inn. We'd like to have dinner locally. So if you could recommend a place with fresh fish. Shrimp. Scallops. Salmon." MR picked up on Sage's distaste. "Something wrong?"

Sage shook her head. Nope. Nothing to see here.

But the ever-probing venture capitalist wouldn't let it go, so Nick placed a comforting hand on Sage's spine. "Sage got sick on shrimp early in her pregnancy. Just thinking about it makes her ill."

An understatement if there ever was one. She couldn't even look at recipes. Never mind photos of the cooked food. And she was a chef! Hopefully, the malady would pass. But for now, a simple whiff made her toss her cookies. Pronto.

"I see," MR said.

When clearly she didn't.

Eager to discuss something other than her continuing battle with morning—or in some cases, evening—sickness, Sage wrote down the name of a bed-and-breakfast located a short distance away. "They have an executive chef that's on par with the best in Dallas, and the menu and wine list to go with. You'll need reservations. But if you tell them you're here to do business with Nick and he recommended it, I'm sure they'll find a way to fit you in this evening."

"Thanks." MR looked grateful.

"No problem," Sage said.

She'd do whatever she could to help Nick.

Short of ruining everything and marrying him, of course.

"MR IS RIGHT," Hope Lockhart said, a short time later, when Sage and Nick went over to her brother and sister-in-law's home. The four of them gathered in the kitchen of the Victorian, while one-year-old Max sat in his high chair and ate his dinner of green beans and diced meatballs.

A crisis manager and public relations expert, Hope had guided the family through several calamities since first meeting them the previous summer. "While there are many customers who won't care whether you or Nick ever tie the knot, there are others who will be up in arms over it," Hope told them gently. "You don't want to lose any potential business right out of the gate. Not if you want this venture to be a success."

"Think of the plus side," Garrett added, from his place at the stove. Winking, he gave the boiling pasta and spaghetti sauce another stir. "Mom will be delighted."

It was all Sage could do not to groan. "Did you all tell her yet?"

Garrett shook his head. "Like we said a while ago at the store, that news is yours to deliver, sis. I just wouldn't wait too long."

"Want to do it now?" Nick asked, as he and Sage turned down an invitation to stay for dinner and left.

The sun had set, leaving the quiet residential street bathed in the yellow glow of the streetlamps. Stars shone overhead.

Feeling the need for some support, Sage tucked her hand in Nick's and rested her chin on the solid warmth of his upper arm. "First, we need to talk about what we're going to do."

He caught her other hand and turned her to face him. "I don't expect you to marry me, Sage."

But clearly, she thought, it was what he wanted. A simple solution to a very thorny problem. "You heard what MR said. If we don't, your deal with her firm is likely off."

Nick shrugged, a distant look coming into his eyes. Sage felt about a million miles away from him. She didn't like it. In an effort to understand what was going on with him, she asked, "Did you ever tell MR you felt trapped here in Laramie?"

His broad shoulders tensed. "Not in so many words."

"So she inferred it?"

He nodded curtly.

Which had to mean, she knew Nick pretty well. Pushing aside a surge of unexpected jealousy, Sage gently pushed for more information. "Why would she do that? What did you tell her?" *That you haven't told me?*

"When I first approached Metro Equity Partners we talked a lot about the fact that the store, the custom boot-making operation and the ranch have been in my family for four generations. The fact that the women have always run the mercantile operation, the men the ranch."

"But at some point all that changed."

"When my mom and dad died in the accident when I was ten, my oldest sister, Erin, took over everything. She sold off all the cattle, but she ran the store."

"She also raised you and your three older siblings, right?"

Nick nodded gratefully. "Along with her own kids, yeah. But when she married Mac Wheeler and they added a set of twins and another baby to the three they were already raising, Erin needed to take a break from running Monroe's for a while, and just concentrate on her family life and custom boot-making—which she really loves." He released a breath. "So at my suggestion, she spun her custom boot-making operation off into a separate business entity, while I took over at Monroe's. And when she and Mac moved to Amarillo for his work, I put aside my own plans to work for a big corporation in

Dallas or Houston, and stepped in permanently to run things here."

"No one else could do it?"

"It wouldn't have made sense. I was the business major in the family. My brother, Gavin, studied medicine. My twin sisters, Bess and Bridgett, are both nurses. Plus, the three of them all needed to be closer to the hospital and their patients, so while they got places in town, I moved back to the ranch to take care of the horses, too."

This was something he rarely talked about. "Doesn't sound like you had a lot of choice," Sage said.

He shrugged. "I'm the youngest. It's my turn. And the way I figure it, a business is a business. And since my goal is to build Monroe's Western Wear into what it could be—not just what it is—I'm okay with it."

She understood concessions, because she had made more than a few of her own. Often unhappily. Knowing the kind of resentment that could fester, long-term, she asked, "Would you be okay with losing this venture capital deal because of conditions I put on our arrangement?"

His expression inscrutable, he worked his jaw back and forth. "I'll find other investors."

It wasn't that easy. If it had been, she sensed he would have done this five years ago, when he first took over the family business.

She ignored the quiver, low in her belly, her need to comfort him in a very elemental way. "How long did it take you to interest Metro Equity Partners?"

"Eighteen months or so."

Which, Sage knew, could feel like a lifetime when you weren't getting what you wanted. She couldn't bear to see him disappointed. Not when she was getting everything she wanted—primarily, his baby. "It's unacceptable for you to have to go back to square one," she told him firmly.

"It's just the way it is." Shouldering the burden stoically, he exhaled. "After all, we're not talking pennies here."

She recalled what he had shared with her of the proposal, thus far. "We're talking six additional stores, opened two months apart, over the course of a year. We're talking about the many years of work you've already put in on this business plan, which is…"

"Four, give or take."

"Four years." Sage shook her head in silent remonstration, more determined than ever to make him as happy as he'd made her. "You're not giving that up. And you're especially not giving that up on account of me. Got it?"

She tapped his sternum with her index finger.

Vowing softly, "They want you married? We'll get married. ASAP. And it doesn't have to change a thing."

BUT, OF COURSE, Sage quickly learned, matrimony changed everything, in the blink of an eye. Not only was her mother—who'd been frankly disapproving about Sage's initial plans to have a baby on her own via artificial insemination—delighted to hear that Sage was carrying Nick's child, she was even happier when she learned that her daughter was planning to marry him right away.

"That's wonderful news!" Lucille said, tears shimmering in her eyes as she hugged them both. "But, pregnant or not, you need to do this right—"

Meaning have a big fancy wedding, Sage thought in consternation.

"—and make this a special day reflective of your enduring love for each other," Lucille finished firmly.

Except, she thought with a wince, that would make the nuptials feel real, and she and Nick knew they weren't.

At least not the way her mother was assuming, since she hadn't told Lucille why they were suddenly heading to the altar. And she had made Hope and Garrett promise they wouldn't, either.

"If you want me to call my event planner," Lucille continued, already reaching for her phone, "I'll get right on it."

Sage gently touched Lucille's forearm. "Actually, Mom, I think Nick and I want to make all the decisions ourselves."

"All right," her mother conceded, smiling at Sage's rounded tummy. "But if you, or Nick, or the baby need me—"

"We know where to find you," she promised.

"Well, that went okay," Nick said, when they left the Circle H Ranch.

Sage savored the intimacy of being alone with Nick. She loved the steadfast way he always backed her up. "Mom's always up for more grandchildren." There were four now, and with two of her four siblings married, another engaged, hints of more to soon be on the way.

Looking as if he wouldn't want to be anywhere else, Nick drove the country roads with the same masculine ease he did everything else. "This is going to work out," he told her reassuringly, then took her hand and kissed the back of it.

Tingling all over for no reason she could figure, Sage looked over at him. "Are you sure you don't feel trapped?"

He dropped his hold on her hand. "No." Steering the car over to the berm, he put it in Park and turned to look at her. His glance sifted slowly over her face, lingering on the flush in her cheeks and her bare lips, before returning slowly to her eyes. Sage caught her breath. As their gazes locked, he rubbed a strand of her hair between his fingers. The corners of his lips curved upward. "Do you?"

Insides quivering, Sage took a moment to consider. At times like this, all she wanted to do was make love with him. Maybe because that was the one place where they felt the closest.

"Yes. No. I don't know?" she said honestly at last, meeting his playful smile with one of her own. Taking off her seat belt, she moved to wrap her arms around his broad shoulders and kiss him. "But if this will help you make all your business dreams come true," she promised tenderly, wanting to give him as much as he had given her, "I'm all for it…"

"Good to know," Nick replied, a sexy rumble emanating from his broad chest. Taking her all the way into his arms, he covered her mouth with his own. And though she had promised herself she would keep their relationship in the friends-with-benefits category, it was darn near impossible to hold back the rush of feelings inside her as she melted into his embrace. He kissed her like there was no tomorrow. Only today. Like the future would always belong to them if only she had the courage to see where the relationship between them led.

And for the moment that was enough.

More than enough, she thought wistfully. Their plans to keep their nuptials simple, and under their control, quickly went out the window, however, when they met with MR late the next morning.

"You need a big, splashy, over-the-top romantic wedding. With plenty of photos we can release to the press later, if need be. And we need to get it done in three days," the venture capital exec said.

To help with that, MR had summoned her assistant,

Everett Keller, a nerdy-looking young man who was clad in spit-shined wing tips, neatly pressed slacks with suspenders and a starched purple shirt with a wildly patterned bow tie. He hovered nearby, taking notes on an electronic tablet.

Sage's eyes widened in shock. "There's no way we can pull together a wedding in that time frame!"

Nor would she want to do so.

MR arched a perfectly plucked brow. "There is if I call in every favor I'm owed, and you all and your families do the same and we have it at Nick's ranch." She paused to let her words sink in while Everett typed furiously. "Saturday evening is perfect."

Sage and Nick exchanged exasperated looks.

Neither of them liked being railroaded into anything, and MR was being awfully pushy about what was, in the end, a very personal matter.

"Let me put it another way," the elegant redhead stated bluntly. "The partners meet on Monday to hear the presentation and vote on whether or not to fund the initial phase of Nick's proposal. I can't delay the vote on this project without explaining to them why. If I do that, and you're still not married, it's over. Done. On the other hand, if you're married, and wildly in love and expecting a baby, it's not really going to matter. So you decide. You want it done by Saturday evening? Or not?"

Sage looked at Nick.

Once again he wore that poker face. But just for a second, she had seen that flash of disappointment in his eyes. The look he evidenced every time he hit a roadblock in his plans to expand Monroe's Western Wear. It was the same look she'd had whenever her own dreams of having a baby incurred another snafu. The one her ex had worn whenever she talked about getting engaged, when

Terrence was perfectly content with things the way they were. She was not going to be the reason for Nick's unhappiness the way she had been with her ex's.

"We'll do it," she said, forcing herself to match MR's enthusiasm. She turned to Nick, took both his hands in hers and squeezed fiercely. "Just promise me one thing." She looked deep into his eyes. "All of this won't damage our friendship." Because she didn't think she could live without that.

"Come on now, darlin'." He gave her a long, searing look, then wrapped an arm around her shoulders and leaned forward to buss the tip of her nose. "You and I both know I would *never* let that happen."

She heaved a sigh of relief.

Out of the corner of her eye, she saw Everett Keller pause in bemusement. Like he couldn't believe he had to stand around and witness this. MR had an intense, watchful expression on her face, too. Almost as if she were waiting for a time bomb to go off.

Sage hoped it wasn't Nick.

Splaying both her hands across his broad chest, she relaxed into his easy embrace. Met his eyes. He seemed to be taking this all in stride. But was he really? She drew a deep breath, warned, "Preparing for a wedding, even in a normal amount of time, can be really stressful."

She only had to recall Terrence's reaction to their brief engagement to know that.

Nick nodded. Still appearing confident, unperturbed.

So, why, Sage wondered, was *she* suddenly completely on edge?

Again, MR observed the emotion simmering just beneath the surface and stepped in to assist. "That's why Everett and I are here," she soothed. "Not just to help but to make sure that absolutely everything goes according to plan. I promise you both…this is one wedding that will go off without a hitch."

Chapter Three

Sage snuggled against Nick, luxuriating in the safe, warm feel of his big strong body. "It's a good thing we're not getting married today for real, otherwise seeing each other like this would be bad luck."

"How can seeing each other ever be bad luck?" Nick regarded her with a devilish glint in his blue eyes.

Sage inhaled the unique masculine scent of him. On impulse, she kissed his cheek, found her way to his mouth. "You know what I mean."

"I do." He studied her as if he found her as endlessly fascinating as she found him. Stroking a lazy hand down her spine, he confessed huskily, "It's been a crazy three days."

"No kidding." She sighed, her cheek brushing delectably against the sandpapery roughness of his morning beard. She so loved having him in her bed, even though his six-foot-four frame took up so much room they barely fit on the queen-sized mattress.

A problem that, now that she'd entered her second trimester, sometimes left her with a tiny backache. "So many decisions…"

He turned toward her so they had full body contact. Lower still, his hardness pressed against her. "So little time."

A spark of arousal unfurled deep inside her. "We saved some headaches by delegating a lot of them out."

MR had arranged for a justice of the peace friend to preside over the civil ceremony. She'd also provided the caterer, tent and chair setup crew—all within the budget Nick and Sage had set. Assembling the guest list and sending out last minute e-invites had gone to the sisters-in-law, Hope and Adelaide, and the seating chart delegated to Chance's fiancée, Molly. Lucille had been in charge of the flowers and the menu for the reception. While Nick and Sage had selected the DJ and the songs.

This morning, she was going to have the final fitting for her dress—a gown from her cousin Jenna Lockhart's bridal salon—at her mother's ranch while Nick picked up his tuxedo. Her brother Wyatt's wife, Adelaide, was her maid of honor. Nick's brother, Gavin, was best man.

Nick reached for Sage playfully as the first light of dawn fell through the window blinds of her second-floor apartment. "I think we have time to make love one more time…" He kissed her shoulder.

Sage wished. She eased away and went to find a thick fluffy robe to ward off the chill of the late-January morning. "Actually, we don't." Computer tablet in hand, she climbed back into bed. "We haven't written our vows yet."

Reluctant, Nick scowled. "Sure you want to do that?" he asked, practical as ever. "Instead of going with the tried and true?"

The thought of promising to love him until death do them part seemed like tempting fate. Sage swallowed. "Given the fact that we're not…" Her voice trailed off. She didn't know how to finish without insulting him. Or the connection they shared, which she had to admit pretty much defied description.

He studied her, as determined to understand her as she was him. "In love?"

Sage caught his hand in hers, and pressed it against the center of her chest. "Maybe not in the traditional way, but I do love you, Nick. As a friend. A *best* friend."

His expression was as veiled as hers was open. "I adore you, too," he said softly.

She sensed there was more. Unsure, however, as to whether or not she wanted to hear it, she murmured, "Okay, then, that's what we need to say." She settled a pillow across her lap, to use as a desk. Opened up the leather computer tablet case, turned on the attached mini keyboard and logged on.

While she got comfortable, Nick folded his arms behind his head. He lounged against the pillows, his gaze drifting over her lazily. "There's no way I can memorize anything this late in the game. I mean, I'm the kid who always flunked the English class assignments where we had to get up and recite a poem."

Although she was wearing an old-fashioned button-front nightshirt that concealed her baby bump, he was clad only in his boxer briefs. Hence, with the sheet draped low across his abdomen, she had a very nice view of his broad, masculine chest.

Too nice, if she were to remain on task.

"Public speaking pressure?" she teased, turning her gaze away from the sinewy muscle and crisp dark hair that arrowed across his pecs, and narrowed, on the way to the goody trail...

"Procrastinating, and making up excuses, are we?" she taunted.

"Mmm-hmm."

"Not going to cut it, cowboy," she retorted sternly. "We have to get this done. Right now."

His sensual lips compressed as he ran a hand through the tousled layers of his dark hair. "Maybe you should tell me yours."

"I would. Except I haven't written mine yet, either."

His low laughter filled the bedroom. He rubbed a hand beneath the sexy-rough stubble on his jaw. "Aha."

"But I will now." Cuddled up in bed, beside him, sitting against the headboard.

He rested his chin on her shoulder. "This should be interesting."

"I take thee, Nick, for my parent-in-arms?"

He shook his head. "Sounds like we're forming a club."

Sage used the mini keyboard to type in some more. "May the joy that brought us together hold us in good stead through the days ahead."

Nick wrinkled his brow, sexy as ever. "That's going to have people scratching their heads and saying *huh.*"

Sage opened a new document window on the screen. "Okay, Smarty-pants. You try."

He thought a moment. "I don't know what I did to get you to look my way," he drawled finally, "but I'm sure grateful you did."

Sage snickered. "Aren't those song lyrics?"

He grinned back, allowing, "Maybe."

Only able to imagine the grief she'd get from her brothers if they went that route, Sage decreed, "I think we should be a little more original."

Nick's brow rose in annoyance. "Then we should have started this weeks ago."

"Okay," Sage said hastily. "There's no need to get testy. How about I say, 'There are no words to describe how I feel about you. I just know this feels right, and I want to be with you,' or something like that."

Nick tilted his head. "Pretty good. Vague. But truthful."

Sage grinned, glad an argument—which would have been their first—had been averted. "Now all we have to do is add to it. Refine it a little. And then come up with something equally reassuring for you to say, too."

NICK WASN'T SURE who Sage was trying to pacify with this whole writing-their-own-vows stuff, but if it made her feel better, then he was all for it. The hectic nature of the last three days had been hard on her. She looked weary. And that couldn't be good for her or the baby.

So when she declared them done, a short while later, hit the print command and then ran over to her printer to pull out two sheets of paper, one for her and one for him, he celebrated by kissing her again.

One thing led to another.

The next thing they knew she really was late, and so was he. They split up, heading their separate ways. He did not see her again until she walked down the aisle on her eldest brother Garrett's arm.

As she glided toward him, looking like a princess out of some Disney movie, his heart caught in his chest. She was so damn gorgeous in that ball gown–style wedding dress. So sweet and innocent and glowing. He felt like the luckiest man in the world. And would have even if she hadn't been carrying his child and on the verge of giving him the family of his own he had always wanted.

"Who giveth the bride away?" the JP asked.

Garrett lifted Sage's veil, kissed her cheek and answered, "Her family and I do."

Sage's lower lip quivered.

In that second, Nick realized what a disservice he had done. This was hard enough without his deceased parents and her late father here to see this. But to secretly be doing it all for a business deal… He swore silently to himself as he took her hand, vowing he would make it up to her. Some way. Somehow.

The distinguished-looking sixtysomething justice of the peace welcomed everyone to their nuptials. He spoke briefly about the grave responsibility entailed in entering into a marriage.

A speech that only made Nick feel all the guiltier.

"And now we will turn it over to Nick and Sage, who have written their own vows. Sage, would you like to go first?"

She nodded, hands trembling as she unfolded the page. Looking down, she began reading nervously, "Nick. There are no watercress…"

A few smothered chuckles.

The justice of the peace gave everyone a sharp look.

Aware of the solemnity of the occasion, everyone fell silent once again.

Sage shook her head, her brow pleating worrisomely as she squinted. "Sorry. There are no *words* that would adequately describe how I feel about you, Nick." She looked up with a smile, then read confidently from the paper in her hand, "So, I'm just going to say, I think yeast…"

Another undercurrent of nervous giggles.

Sage blushed.

Nick slid a hand beneath her forearm to steady her, aware she wouldn't be the first bride to wilt from a combination of nerves, and in their case, guilt. Resolved to help her through this, he encouraged under his breath, "Just calm down. You got this."

Sage nodded. Jerking in a deep breath, tried again. "I think *you* are the most wonderful mango…" She looked up, clearly mortified. "I mean, *man* I've ever known. And…" She swiftly scanned the page, looking even more distressed. "I think I'm going to just say I'm really happy to be marrying you today. And *stop* right there."

Radiating embarrassment, she gestured at him. "On to you."

Nick had never known Sage to fall apart like this. But given how quickly everything had happened, he figured she was entitled to suffer the same kind of public speaking phobia that had haunted him as a kid, and cut her speech short.

With a grin, he removed the paper from the inner pocket of his tuxedo jacket and unfolded it. Still holding her eyes, wordlessly promising that he would make this okay for both of them with the best recitation he had ever given in his life, he looked down at his vows. And began. "Sage. You are the most brioche…" He stopped and shook his head while trying to quickly remember what should have been there.

If this is what "his bride" had been dealing with, no wonder she'd panicked!

Ignoring the faint titters in their audience, he tried again. "The most um…most…*beautiful* woman I've ever met, inside and out."

Whew! High five on that one!

"And if there is one thing today is going to show us," he continued determinedly, glad to be back on track, "it's that we will otters have each other."

Otters?

What the hell?

And then, amid the muffled rumble of new laughter, he realized what had happened. There was no need to go on reading from the pages Sage had printed out for them. Not unless they wanted this to turn into even more of a comedy skit.

He turned to face their guests and held up the page for everyone to see. "So much for writing our vows on an electronic device with autocorrect," he announced, grinning from ear to ear. "Seriously, folks—" getting into the spirit of the hilarity he crumpled it up dramatically, and tossed it to one of his sisters in the front row "—proofread!"

With a mischievous grin, Sage crumpled up her vows, and tossed 'em to family, too.

Taking both his bride's hands in his he made an executive decision and decided, "We're just going to have to do this on the fly."

Ignoring her prior worry about the results of any extemporaneous speech, he paused and looked deep into her eyes, then said what had been on his mind since the day they'd decided to risk this.

"I used to think that life had to be lived in stages. If I was going to have a family, I needed to find someone compatible and get married right out of college." He paused ruefully, to let his prior idiocy sink in. "A plan that did not work for so many reasons..."

He hadn't been anywhere mature enough. Hadn't known the first thing about love. Might still not...at least when it came to the traditional variety.

Aware the world had shrunk to just the two of them, he looked deep into her eyes and continued, "And then, and only then, would I focus on my career goals. Secure the future. And when that was all set, then I could have kids."

Understanding lit her eyes. She'd had similar expectations. It was one of the things that had drawn them together.

"But despite my ambition, it didn't work out that way.

And I began to think that my work dreams and goals were all I was going to have." His throat tightened unexpectedly. He forced himself to go on hoarsely. "Then I met you, Sage, and I realized things didn't have to happen in any specific time frame or in any particular order. We could be friends. And then more than friends. And now parents-to-be of the no doubt most amazing child who will ever be born in Laramie County!"

Laughter rippled through the attendees as the world around them crowded in once again.

Happiness roaring through him with the force of a white-water river, he squeezed her hands and said, "In the seven months we've known each other, you've brought so much happiness to my life, I can imagine just how fantastic the rest of our time together will be. And darlin', I can't wait to experience it all with you," he finished soberly, a lump rising in his throat.

BECAUSE SHE COULD see Nick meant every single word he said, Sage's eyes misted over, too.

Grinning, she continued to hold on to him as fiercely as he was holding on to her. "Okay, cowboy." She heaved a sigh of relief. "If you get a do over with our vows, so do I! So here goes…" Taking comfort in the encouragement his steady regard offered, she jerked in a bolstering breath. "I never thought after everything that happened to me leading up to this point that I would want to be involved again." *Or risk a relationship that could stomp my soul to pieces.*

"But then I met you, and everything changed for me, too. I wanted friendship." *Deep, abiding, tell-each-other-almost-everything friendship that was eventually supplemented by deliciously sensual, mind-blowing passion.*

"And then, a baby, and now here we are getting married," she exclaimed excitedly.

Her nerves calmed as she went on. "We've laid the right groundwork."

The corners of his lips quirked up in a way that let her know he could not have agreed more with her assessment.

Their eyes still locked, Sage pushed on, promising Nick, "We're going to have a happy life together. And when our baby gets here at some point close to Father's Day—" an astonishing present in and of itself "—you're right, we're going to be even happier than either of us ever dreamed."

Nick leaned in as if to kiss her.

Her heart fluttered.

The JP clamped a restraining hand on Nick's shoulder. "Whoa, there, pardner. We're not done yet. We've still got the rings and the official pronouncement to go."

Nick grunted, his lips hovering just above hers, then reluctantly drew back.

"You're right," he said finally to one and all, as everyone smiled and laughed yet again. "We've definitely got to get this done right."

No kidding, Sage thought.

This was beginning to feel like a whole lot more than the extension of their previous arrangement that they had privately agreed it would be.

Following their purposefully abbreviated next steps, Nick slid the wedding ring on Sage's finger. "Sage, I take thee to be my lawful wedded wife."

Sage followed suit and put a simple gold band on Nick's left hand. "Nick, I take thee to be my lawful wedded husband," she said.

"Then by the power vested in me," the JP said finally, "I pronounce you husband and wife."

Nick gathered her in his arms.

As he kissed her, a roar of approval went up, matched only by the relief and joy whisking through Sage.

SEVERAL HOURS LATER, Sage stared in the master suite bathroom mirror. "You really think my tiara is crooked?"

Lucille shook her head, tears abruptly misting her eyes. "No. I just wanted a moment alone with you before the evening ended."

"Oh, Mom." Sage turned and gave her mother a hug. This was a big day for both of them. All of it happening a little too fast for comfort.

On the other hand, had they had more time to consider, Sage wasn't sure she would've been able to go through with it. Because, no matter how fond she and Nick were of each other, at the end of the day, it all felt a little dishonest.

Lucille perched on the edge of Nick's bed and patted the place next to her.

Carefully arranging the poofy skirt of her wedding gown, Sage settled beside her mother. "What is it?" she asked softly.

"I just wanted to tell you how happy I am for you tonight."

"You mean that?"

Lucille nodded. "I confess, I had my doubts when you told me you and Nick were going to get married. I thought it all might have been related to his business somehow. Especially when the venture capitalist he's been working with—"

"MR Rhodes."

"—and her assistant, Everett Keller, became so involved in the execution of the wedding plans."

Sage tamped down her guilt. It was bad enough she

and Nick were being disingenuous. They did not need to bring anyone else into it who wasn't already. "We kind of needed everyone to pitch in to make this happen, Mom."

"I know, and MR and Everett have both been wonderful, as has everyone."

"But...?"

Lucille worried the diamond necklace around her neck. The one Sage's father had given her mother for their fortieth wedding anniversary. "I'm just concerned you and Nick were going into this the same way you did having a baby together. Hastily and without forethought."

Her mother's elegant brow furrowed. "And that feeling was confirmed when the two of you started your wedding vows. But—" she paused, shaking her head "—then you started speaking what was in your hearts. The way you looked at each other—with such tenderness, faith and affection—I knew those feelings the two of you have worked so hard to keep private are genuine."

Lucille took Sage's hands in hers. "Bottom line...your dad would have been *so proud* of you tonight."

But would he really have?

Sage was still worrying about that throughout her and Nick's final dance of the evening.

Still wondering if she and Nick had done the right thing after all, when he pressed a kiss in her hair and then drew back to look down at her tenderly.

"Ready for one last surprise?" he asked huskily.

Chapter Four

Sage looked at Nick in much the same way he imagined he had looked, half an hour earlier, when he had received the news.

"A honeymoon?" she repeated as if she couldn't possibly have heard him right.

He continued slow dancing with her. She felt so good in his arms, and he lamented the fact that their just-best-friends-slash-lovers rules had made this romantic activity off-limits, until now. "Three nights at The Mansion, in Dallas."

Sage drew in a shuddering breath. "One of the most romantic hotels in the city."

So he'd been informed. "It's a gift from Metro Equity Partners. MR told me about it a few minutes ago. The limo is out in the drive. Your brothers are decorating it with the Just Married stuff now."

Sage winced. "Not tin cans."

"And the obligatory sign designating us as newlyweds," he told her with barely checked amusement.

As the last song stopped, so did they. She covered her face with her hand, then peered at him through spread fingers. "We're supposed to go tonight?" she asked, aghast.

There was no debating it. She looked dead on her feet.

Belatedly, he realized what a long few days it had been for her, in her pregnant state. They'd both been going since well before dawn. To expect her to endure another two-and-a-half-hour drive was probably way out of line. "We can wait until tomorrow," he soothed. "Drive there ourselves. Check in then."

Sage looked tempted, but remained careful of his feelings and commitments as always. "How is that going to be perceived?"

Hard to say, since he had yet to meet most of the partners who would be voting on his proposal.

"You know what, forget I even said that." Sage squared her slender shoulders, as if she were going into battle. "It's never a good idea to look a gift horse in the mouth. Particularly when you have the biggest business deal of your life pending."

Bless her generous heart. "You're sure you want to do this?"

She nodded, then said with her newfound practicality, "What's the alternative, anyway? Go back to our original plan, spend the night in my apartment and forego any celebration of our nuptials?" She rose on tiptoe and whispered seductively in his ear, "If we go to Dallas, at least we'll have our privacy."

Given the scrutiny they'd been under all evening, there was definitely something to be said for that.

"WAKE UP, SLEEPYHEAD," Nick murmured in Sage's ear, several hours later.

With effort, she opened her eyes. They were indeed at the luxury hotel. Apparently, she'd slept the entire journey. "What time is it?" she asked, blinking herself awake.

"Two thirty."

He still looked good. More than good, actually, in that dark tuxedo.

She smothered a yawn and tore her eyes from the hard sinew of his chest beneath his snowy white shirt. "Sorry I was such bad company."

He hugged her close, then kissed her temple and the top of her head. "I slept, too."

She drew back slightly and tipped her head up to his. He was definitely wide-awake now. With plenty of energy. The kind that usually presaged incredible lovemaking.

She tingled all over, just thinking about it.

His sexy grin widening, he teased, "Ready for the best part of the entire festivity?"

She placed a hand flirtatiously across her heart. She did not have to pretend to feel swept away. "Oh my."

His low masculine laugh filled the interior of the limo. "Oh my is right." He brought her close for a long lingering kiss, ended only by the intrusion of their driver opening the door. Nick emerged first, then assisted her in getting out, not an easy thing, given the fact that they were still in their wedding finery and the silk chiffon skirt of her dress was poufed enough to disguise her pregnancy. The driver followed them with the bags they had hastily packed before leaving Laramie County. Nick at his ranch house, she at her apartment on her way out of town.

They swept through the lobby, getting grins from everyone who saw them. "Congratulations!" more than one person called out as they signed in.

The bellhop escorted them to their suite and set their suitcases in the bedroom. He returned with a flourish, announcing, "Metro Equity Partners thought you might be in need of a late-night supper. So…" Another uniformed attendant rolled a room service table into the living room.

Silver-domed dishes were placed on an elegantly made-up table for two, next to an ice bucket containing a bottle of exquisite champagne, sparkling water and ginger ale.

Which was good, Sage thought.

Because now that she was awake, she was feeling a little nauseated. She wondered if there were any crackers in the minibar. If not, the elegant dinner rolls in the basket would probably take the edge off.

She smiled appreciatively as Nick tipped the attendants. "Seems like the partners have thought of everything."

"Let us know if we can do anything else." The attendants disappeared.

"I don't know about you, but I'm starved," Nick said.

He took off the lids with a flourish.

The roasted filet mignon and butter poached lobster tail had her feeling a little iffy, but it was the garlic prawns with Cajun aioli that really sent Sage over the edge.

"Sage, come on, open the door."

She leaned over the toilet bowl, arms folded over the cool porcelain. "No."

"I sent all the fish away."

She closed her eyes against the husky rumble of his voice. "You didn't have to do that."

"Ah, actually, Sage? I kind of think I did."

How could he maintain his sense of humor when she had just ruined everything? She moaned again, in even more distress. "I'm sorry."

The other door that opened up off the bedroom, the one she hadn't time or foresight to lock, swung inward. Nick strolled in. "What do you have to be sorry about?" He knelt down beside her.

He cupped a hand beneath her chin, and regarded her

tenderly. "You're pregnant. I'm the one who should have thought to ask what was in there first, before lifting the room service domes and treating you to all those aromas."

The memory of the sights and smells made her shudder with distaste.

"I'm guessing it was the shrimp."

"Prawns," she admitted with difficulty. "And yes." My heavens, yes.

He stroked a hand through her hair—or tried—the elegantly upswept curls were still heavily lacquered into place. "I've seen people throw up before, you know." He wet a washcloth with cool water, wrung it out and placed it on the back of her neck.

She wallowed in her misery. "You haven't seen me."

He gazed at her possessively. "If we're living together, that is going to change."

What was he talking about? Sage sat back on her haunches and stared at him. "Living together?" she repeated.

"Well—" he shrugged, pausing to get comfortable, too "—now that we're married, I figured we'd spend the night together whenever I am in town, and then when the baby comes, and I don't have to travel so much…"

As much as Sage wanted to lean on him then, the way she was now, she wasn't sure it was a good idea. "You know this isn't a real marriage." More like a convenient arrangement. For business reasons.

"It can still be any kind of union we want it to be."

Why did he have to look so sexy? Especially under these circumstances? He should be irritated. Repelled. Not ready to move in with her!

Proceeding cautiously, she asked, "What kind of union do you want it to be?"

Mischief twinkled in his deep blue eyes. "The kind where we have a lot of great sex."

Sage rolled her eyes. "You would say that now." *When I've just finished throwing up and feel and look like death warmed over.*

Chivalrously, Nick helped her to her feet. "And have long talks," he said. "The kind that last all night."

She could go with that. It was what brought them together in the first place.

Tilting her head to study him closely, she murmured, "Or times when we say nothing at all, and it's still okay."

"Sounds good to me."

Shakily, she headed for her suitcase to get her toiletries bag. Nick stood by, ready to help if need be, as she removed her toothpaste and brush and then returned to the bathroom. Still fighting residual waves of nausea, Sage tried not to think how intimate this all was. "What else?"

He lounged a short distance away as she brushed her teeth, then handed her a towel. "I'd like to know we could be apart and still do our own thing and still be okay."

Sage blotted her mouth. "We will be."

He smoothed a stray curl from her cheek and admitted softly, "And I'd like to think that when the baby comes, we'll also enjoy spending lots of time together as a family, as we adjust to those new roles."

Strangely enough, she'd been able to picture that from the first, even before they'd made love or she asked him to father their child.

Sage glanced in the mirror, noting her tiara really was askew. She wondered for how long it had been. Perching on the cushioned stool, she began working the pins out of her upswept hair.

When she still couldn't get the glittering headpiece free, he moved to help her. His fingers moving gently in her hair, he worked it out and then set it on the bathroom counter. "What about you?" he asked gruffly. "What kind of parameters do you think our marriage should have?"

"I guess I want pretty much what we had before. We're only together when we want to be. We don't owe each other phone calls. Or have to check in. Or feel in any other way constrained. What is yours is yours, what is mine is mine."

The smile on his lips reached his eyes. "Except for this baby we're having."

"Which is *ours*," Sage agreed wholeheartedly.

A comfortable silence fell.

"Feeling better now?" Nick asked.

Not exactly. But rather than dwell on the ever-present queasiness, Sage drew a deeply constrained breath and gestured at the formfitting bodice. "I will be as soon as I get out of this damn petticoat and dress."

He laughed, low and deep. "I think I can help you with that."

Unfortunately, no sooner had he started to ease the zipper down, than Sage felt that unmistakable urge to be sick. Again.

Hand to his chest, she shoved him back out of the bathroom, and slammed the door in his face.

And was sick, sick, sick…

Finally, the retching stopped.

Some honeymoon, Sage thought miserably, still hugging the porcelain.

This time Nick didn't ask to come in.

As soon as the commode flushed, he opened the door and walked in. All big protective male. "Your stomach empty?"

Sage nodded weakly. "I think so."

Once again, he assisted her to her feet. "You need to go to bed."

"Nick…"

He rolled his eyes. "Not for that, sweetheart. For some much-needed sleep." He turned her around. Eased the rest of the zipper down, and assisted her out of the skirt and petticoat.

His brows lifted appreciatively at her sexy wedding lingerie. Sage hadn't thought it necessary at the time. Although what else she would have worn under such a romantic dress, she did not know.

Now, however, if they hadn't been dealing with the catastrophe of evening sickness, she could see where it would have come in handy.

But certainly not now.

Once again, he rushed to her aid. He grabbed a thick and fluffy white spa robe from the hanger in the bathroom, eased her arms into it, then guided her to the bed.

Appreciating the warmth and softness of the garment, almost as much as she appreciated his kindness, Sage wrapped it around her. "Could you do me a favor and see if you can find me some saltines?"

"Sure thing." He looked in the minibar, then slammed it shut. "Be right back." He eased out of the hotel room.

She changed into her light-blue-and-white floral pajamas, then climbed beneath the bed covers.

It took fifteen minutes and a personal visit with the manager to the room service kitchen, but Nick rushed back with a big bowl of crisp saltine crackers, and another bottle of chilled ginger ale in hand. Only to find Sage curled up in the big hotel bed, fast asleep.

Aware, despite everything, that this was one of the best days of his entire life, he got ready for bed and climbed in beside her, wrapping her in his arms.

She snuggled against him.

The next thing Nick knew the bedside phone was ringing. Loudly.

Sage moaned in distress. He felt the same.

He reached across her to answer it, thinking this better be good. "Yep?"

"Nick, MR."

What the...

"Who is it?" Sage slid up on her elbows, looking so delectably tousled he had to tamp down the desire to make love to her then and there.

She blinked furiously. "Is anything wrong?" she continued.

"Our families are all fine," Nick immediately reassured Sage. So far as he knew, anyway.

Still struggling to wake up, he rubbed the sleep from his eyes, asked, "What's going on, MR?"

"My assistant and I are in the lobby."

A lot of words went through Nick's mind. None of them pleasant. He shoved a hand through his hair. "Why?"

"We need to talk. Can we come up?"

Only able to imagine how his new wife might take such an intrusion, Nick said gruffly, "It might be better if I came down there."

Sage shook her head, grabbed his arm. As always, not one to put herself first. "It's fine," she mouthed and slipped from the bed.

Nick swore silently. There went his plans to really pamper Sage this morning. Make up for the horrendous sickness the night before.

Figuring they might as well get whatever-this-was over with, he ordered tersely, "Come on up."

He had just finished dressing when the knock sounded outside the suite. Barefoot, angry, he walked to the door.

"Yeah?" he said, as MR brushed by him, Everett in

tow. Both were clad in the type of business attire they usually wore. While Sage had come out of the bathroom and was standing there in her pajamas and robe.

She'd brushed her hair, or tried. Whatever they had done to it before the wedding had left it a glorious curly mess. Her cheeks were bright pink, too, although he sensed that was as much from embarrassment as anything else.

MR looked stunned. "You were still asleep?"

Nick wrapped his arm protectively about Sage's waist. "It's barely nine in the morning." And given the fact that Sage hadn't stopped throwing up until almost 4:00 a.m., hell, yes, they were still asleep!

MR said, "We have a partner meeting tomorrow afternoon to prepare for."

As if he could forget. Still…

He had just gotten married last night.

Even if it was, to his regret, purely for business purposes.

The business proposal for Metro Equity Partners, on the other hand, was something they had been fine-tuning for months.

Nick felt Sage slip away and move to a chair to sit down. "You want to do that now?" It was an effort to remain professional.

MR nodded briskly. "At the office. Sage can stay here, of course."

"How long do you think it will take?" He worked to keep the irritation out of his voice.

"Until we're finished." MR shrugged. "I didn't think this would be a problem, since you only married so this deal would go through."

"It's not," Sage returned shortly. "Take care of business. You don't need to worry about me."

MR brightened. "Thank you for your professionalism, Sage."

"We've got a car and driver on standby to take you wherever you would like to go today," Everett said.

For Sage, that decision seemed easy. "Then I'd like to go home. To Laramie, Texas."

Disappointment roiled through him.

The last thing they needed was to start their marriage off on the wrong foot, as this certainly would.

Nick pivoted to Sage, determined to salvage what they could. "Look, I know it's not ideal. But you could go back to bed now, get some more sleep. Maybe go shopping or to a movie this afternoon. Or enjoy some of the spa services the hotel offers." He paused to let his suggestion sink in. "And we could still have dinner tonight."

FOR A MOMENT, Sage was tempted. She and Nick'd had so little time together over the past few days prepping for their nuptials, and their wedding night had been a total bust. She had been hoping to make up for it this morning, to leave them both with better memories.

But before she could agree to his proposal, MR cut in briskly. "I'm not so sure about your being back in time for an intimate dinner, Nick. But Sage could join us at the office for our meetings. That is—" she turned back to Sage "—if Nick is okay with your knowing that much about his business."

This was becoming way too complicated, Sage thought. Furthermore, she did not want to put him on the spot. She'd rather leave things as they were. With him sharing whatever he liked about his work situation, and no more.

Plus, she sensed his "work session" with MR and Everett, would go better without anyone else present to distract them. So, reluctantly, even though she sort of felt like a coward for deserting him, she bailed.

"Honestly, Nick," she fibbed, "I just want to go back to my apartment."

He pulled her aside, the concern in his eyes almost as thrilling as his sexy presence. "You're sure about this?"

Her heart pounding, even as her spirits sank, Sage nodded. "I have to work tomorrow. So do you. So…I really do have to go back."

Noting he seemed ready to argue, she curved a hand around his forearm. "This proposal is important, Nick." She looked deep into his eyes. "You need to be here with MR and Everett to prepare for the pitch. And be ready for any questions the other partners might have."

MR nodded her approval. "When do you want to leave?"

"Ten minutes?" Sage returned.

She slipped back into the bathroom, bag in tow, washed her face and brushed her teeth, and put on her jeans, shirt and boots.

"I'll walk you down," Nick said when she was ready.

The last thing Sage wanted was an emotional goodbye. And given the way she was feeling…she was just pregnant enough, just hormonal and disappointed enough, to burst into tears at the slightest provocation. So, she faked courage she couldn't begin to feel. "Not to worry, cowboy." She slipped her bag over her shoulder and looped her wedding dress over her arm. "I've got this."

"Actually…" Everett stepped in dutifully to take her suitcase. "I've got it."

Was it her imagination or did Nick look as torn as she felt inside about her leaving? Enough to ask her—once again—to stay? Because if he had…

Oblivious to her secret yearning, he leaned over to kiss her brow and promised instead, "I'll call you."

Not trusting herself to speak, Sage merely nodded, then slipped out the door.

Once again, she got a lot of looks as she walked through the lobby, her wedding finery folded over her arm.

This time, none of them were envious.

Maybe because her mood wasn't exactly celebratory.

Luckily, the town car was waiting at the curb, as promised. Everett held the door for her, while the driver set her bag in the trunk. As the chauffeur climbed behind the wheel, Everett motioned for Sage to roll her window down.

She obliged. MR's trusted assistant paused, still looking young in the face, but suddenly much, much older in the eyes. Like he had seen too much. "You seem like a really nice person," he said at last.

Perplexed, Sage smiled. What was going on here?

She shrugged. "I hope so."

He seemed to struggle with something. Finally, he looked her right in the eye and said, "Everyone is going to tell you that you gained a husband last night."

She kind of had, Sage thought. Although no one but she and Nick knew just how unconventional their arrangement was.

"But that's not what happened," Everett continued.

Sage sensed a warning underlying his low, almost cordial tone. It was as if he knew something she didn't. Her pulse skittering, she pulled herself together and asked nervously, "Then what did?"

He sobered even more. "You lost your best friend."

Shock reverberated through her. "Nick?" she repeated in disbelief.

The young man nodded pityingly, the grimness of his conviction making her lose her breath.

"And don't let anyone tell you any different." He stepped back and, before she could ask him to clarify further, directed the driver to go.

Chapter Five

"Hey," Luisa Vasquez said, stopping in shock as she walked through the back door to The Cowgirl Chef kitchen Sunday evening to get a jump start on the baking for the following day. As usual, the gifted baker was wearing a denim skirt, T-shirt and sneakers, and had her long inky black hair in a French braid. "What are you doing here? I thought you weren't going to be back from your honeymoon for a couple of days."

Sage tried not to blush. "Neither Nick nor I can afford to take that much time off right now."

"You sure?" her assistant manager said. "Because I can handle things here for as long as necessary. It's not like I don't know all your recipes by heart. Or have enough help to carry us."

Sage knew that. She had hired two full-time baristas to handle the coffee and tea machines, another part-time bakery chef in addition to herself and Luisa, and four rotating cashiers/waitstaff, who arranged their hours around family responsibilities and/or college classes. All together, they were quite a team.

"I'm not planning to stay much longer." Sage cut rich and buttery triple-berry scone dough into wedges, and put them on parchment paper–lined baking sheets that would go in the walk-in until morning, when they'd be freshly baked.

Luisa took over rolling out the buttermilk biscuit dough. She eyed Sage carefully. "Nick doesn't mind?"

"He's working, too. In Dallas."

Silence fell. "You sure you're okay?"

"Why wouldn't I be?"

"Post-wedding blues. I had them when I married Carlos."

Sage put the ready-to-bake goods in the walk-in and began spooning out the nutrition-packed breakfast cookies. "That's hard to believe." She sent her assistant an admiring glance. "Sixteen years, six kids later, and you two are still so much in love."

So much so, in fact, they almost made Sage think happily-ever-after endings were possible for couples, after all.

"I know. But back then—" Luisa shook her head ruefully "—when we returned from our honeymoon, which was only a couple of days, and moved into our first home, which was in dire need of renovation, I hit the wall, hard. I kept thinking, is this all there is?"

Sage understood that. It was exactly how she felt right now.

"Plus—" Luisa sighed "—we had wedding bills that had to be paid so Carlos and I were both pulling extra shifts. It was tough going for a while."

Sage observed, "You seem to have recovered nicely."

Luisa gave her a brief hug. "And you will, too, *if* that's all it is."

Despair coiled within Sage, but outwardly she shrugged. "What else could it be?"

Luisa squinted. "Why don't you tell me?"

Sage knew she had to tell someone her fear or she

would burst. She helped Luisa cut out mini rounds for the quiches she was preparing and press them into individual pans. "Can I ask you something?"

"Always."

"You and Carlos are more than husband and wife. You're best friends, aren't you?"

"Have been from the first day we met," Luisa said proudly. "It's one of the things that makes our marriage so strong."

Sage bit her lip. "You don't think that could ever change?"

"No. Why? Are you worried your friendship with Nick might?"

Sage paused. "I want to believe nothing could ever endanger the bonds Nick and I have forged over the last seven months. And that with time, our relationship will only grow stronger…"

But Everett's partings words that morning bothered her.

She still couldn't figure out why MR's assistant had felt the need to warn her as she left Dallas. The efficient, fashionably dressed young man had not struck her as a busybody. Rather, the opposite. Which made his behavior seem all the weirder. Since he really didn't know her or Nick.

Sage knew she should let it go, the way she would have any other attempts to meddle in her life.

And she tried.

All night Sunday, and most of Monday, while working at The Cowgirl Chef. She was still trying that evening when her mother stopped by her apartment around dinnertime, a couple of stray wedding gifts in hand.

Sage thanked her and set them on the counter.

Looking as gorgeous as usual in one of her stylish outfits, Lucille eyed the stacks of yet-to-be-opened presents. "You haven't looked at *any* of those yet?"

"I'm waiting for Nick." But the truth was, it felt almost dishonest opening them, given the reason why she and Nick had tied the knot.

Her mom glanced around. "Where is he?"

"Meetings in Dallas."

Lucille blinked. "That couldn't have been delayed?"

Sage shrugged. "There was no reason to do so."

Lucille worried the pearls around her neck. "How about the fact that the two of you just got married less than forty-five hours ago?"

"It's just business, Mom."

Scoffing, Lucille returned, "That's what your father used to say to me."

Sage folded her arms in front of her, resentment like a river running through her. "I don't remember you complaining at the time." Her dad's devotion to the hedge fund he created had allowed them all to live a life of luxury.

Lucille's gaze turned troubled. "Maybe I should have. Frank didn't have nearly enough time with me or you kids when you all were growing up."

Sage knew that, too. And lamented it. But since there was nothing that could be done about it now, she tried to look on the bright side. "He made up for it the last few years of his life, Mom." In fact, their whole family had grown closer during her dad's illness.

"I know," Lucille said softly. "And I'm glad he had that opportunity to really get to know each and every one of you before his heart gave out completely. But it would have been better if he'd been present more when you were little, too."

A lump formed in Sage's throat. She had missed her

dad at the wedding. She missed him now. She suspected her mother did, too. She moved in to give her mother a brief, reassuring hug. "Nick's going to be a good father, Mom."

Lucille returned the hug, then stepped back to look her in the eye. "But what kind of husband is he going to be?"

Another good question. One, she felt, because of the deal she and Nick had made to maintain independent lives, that she shouldn't even be asking herself. Sage's phone rang. She smiled when she saw the caller ID. "Speak of my handsome husband! There's Nick now…"

Lucille patted her arm. "I'll let you talk to him, dear. But when you're finished, if you want to have dinner at the ranch with the rest of the family tonight, come on out."

Sage nodded and put the phone to her ear.

Lucille left.

"Hey," Sage said, wishing for a moment she had gone against instinct and stayed on in Dallas for a few days, so she could be with Nick now.

He chuckled warmly. "Hey, yourself."

The sexy rumble of his voice did funny things to her insides. Immediately, she felt both better—and more hopelessly lonely, too. Which again was something she had promised herself she would not do—tie her happiness to someone else's presence in her life.

Attempting to maintain some emotional distance, she asked casually, "How'd it go?"

"They voted yes." Nick's triumph resonated between them.

Sage could not help but smile.

"With some stipulations, of course," he added.

"That's great news!"

In the background, she heard a throat clearing. Then

Everett's distinct voice, "MR wants you to know your reservation has been extended at The Mansion for the rest of the week."

Did that mean Nick wasn't coming back to Laramie? Sage wondered with a stab of disappointment.

She guessed it made sense.

"MR will have my head if you don't get back in there," Everett continued.

Nick said something she couldn't quite catch.

Aware she did not want to be the ball and chain dragging him down, even if they were now "married," she forced herself to sound chipper. "Listen, I can tell you're busy, so I'll let you go."

Unexpected tears pricking her eyes, she ended the call.

The silence in her apartment had never seemed louder.

She sat slumped on the sofa, aware she hadn't felt this bereft since she'd been living with Terrence. Waiting for what seemed an eternity for him to come home from his IT job. Only to have him shovel in the dinner she had so lovingly made for him, get right back on his computer and go back to work, again.

He'd said he was doing it so they could live well, and since he made a lot more money than she did, she had not felt she could complain.

And she never had, not even on the day he had told her he wanted out of their relationship, out of their engagement, out of their living together arrangement.

Because he had felt trapped.

The ironic thing was, she had been trapped, too. Albeit of a situation of her own making. And she had not realized it until Terrence blurted out the truth of what he was thinking and feeling.

She could not go back to that loneliness and misery.

Not with Nick.

Not with anyone.

Furthermore, Sage decided resolutely, she wasn't going to. So she had an evening ahead of her. It was the perfect time to relish the solitude and pamper herself. And, by heavens, she would.

THREE HOURS LATER, Sage was deep into relaxation. Conditioner slathered in her freshly shampooed hair, pore-cleaning face mask on, she settled down on the sofa with a pint of Blue Bell's Rocky Road and a spoon.

And that was when the knock sounded. Figuring it was one of her brothers, sent by her mother to check on her, she shouted, "Go. Away."

Another knock.

She ignored it and turned up the volume on the TV instead.

A more persistent knock. Followed by what she thought might have been "Sage!" although it was hard to tell, the sound on the program she was watching was so loud.

More knocking.

Sage sighed and closed her eyes. "I don't need—" *or want*, she added silently "—company!" she shouted again.

This time the lock clicked.

Only a few people had keys to her place.

Her mother.

And…

Oh, no no no no no!

The door swung open.

Nick stood framed in the portal, wearing a Hugo Boss suit and tie. Which was odd. She'd never seen him dress city slick. But then, he'd never been pitching a deal to a venture capital group, either. Although his expression was maddeningly inscrutable, she'd never felt so utterly embarrassed.

Seeing each other at their absolute worst had never been part of their arrangement.

It was all fun, fun, fun!

At least until she had become pregnant. Then, there had been a few all-too-real moments. Crowned by her wedding night hurling episode. Which, she was sure, even though he had been utterly decent about it, had left him feeling "charmed."

And now, to follow that humiliation, with this?

Oh, my heavens. He was never going to want to make love with her again.

And what woman in her right mind could blame him?

Doing her best to appear casual, Sage leaned forward and set her ice cream and spoon on the coffee table in front of her. Belatedly aware the neck of her thick white spa robe was gaping, she pulled it closed at her nape. Great. Now, he probably guessed she was naked beneath the robe, too. Something he might not have known, given the thickness of the terry cloth, if she had not just flashed him.

She regarded him coolly, doing her best to hide her mortification. "What are you doing here?"

An affable grin splitting his handsome face, he shut the door behind him and sauntered across the width of the living room. "I came to see you."

Despite her efforts to contain it, her temper rose. "Well, you can't—" she waved an airy hand "—not when I'm in the middle of all this."

"Too late." His gaze drifted to the wedding gown hanging from the bedroom door, still waiting to go to the specialty cleaners, then he chuckled and yanked loose the knot of his tie. Unfastened the first two buttons on his shirt. "I already have." He sank down beside her on the sofa, to her relief appearing more friend than unexpected "husband" at the moment. He made a perplexed face. "What's the stuff in your hair?"

Didn't the guy have three sisters? Surely, they had used it. "Deep conditioner," Sage enunciated clearly.

His eyes tracked lower to the aqua-green substance now hardening on her face. Lifted an inquisitive brow.

Was she going to have to explain everything? Lord help her, now she was really going to lose her temper.

"A face mask," she said even more clearly.

He kicked off his Italian loafers—another thing she had never seen him wear. "Hmm."

As always, he smelled like soap and man and sun-warmed leather and spice.

He also needed a shave.

Although the rim of evening shadow on his jaw made him look faintly dangerous, in the pirate-about-to-ravish-a-fair-maiden way.

Sage didn't know whether to nudge him with her elbow for showing up unannounced—or kiss him for showing up. How was it he always knew when she needed to see him and be with him? Even when she said she didn't?

Finding refuge in their repartee, she propped an elbow on her hip and echoed wryly, "Hmm? That's all you've got to say?"

He paused to get more comfortable, stretching his long legs over her coffee table. "Well, I could tell you that you look fetching…" He grinned, folding his hands behind his head. "And you kind of do…in a sort of unwrap-the-present-to-discover-just-what's-underneath way…"

She imagined he did want to get her naked.

As much as she wanted to wait—until the usual barriers around her heart were firmly resurrected. Still, it was time for the mask to come off.

She shook her head at him. Rose wordlessly, disappeared into the bathroom and removed the face mask.

Her face pink and glowing, she walked back into the living room.

"What happened to the weeklong reservation at The Mansion?" she asked curiously, aware she still had nothing on beneath her robe.

And suspected he still knew it, too.

"Canceled."

Needing to do something besides throwing herself into his arms, or worse, inviting him into the shower with her, Sage picked up the ice-cream container, took one last bite of Rocky Road, then offered him the same. "You're not going to be in Dallas?"

Smiling appreciatively, he savored the decadent mixture of chocolate, nuts and marshmallow on his tongue. Then handed the spoon back. "At the end of the week, but I'm not going to be staying at that hotel."

"Why not?" she asked, curious.

"Way too expensive. And way too much room for just me."

Sage had grown up with people who turned up their noses at anything but the most elite accommodations. That was one of the things she liked about Nick, the fact that he could be so practical and down-to-earth. Jealousy clenched inside her. "What did MR say to that?"

A few days ago, he'd been worried about offending the venture capital folks.

Nick sobered. "She understands that under normal circumstances I prefer to make my own arrangements. Even if she and her partners are picking up the tab for all travel, per our agreement.

"The only reason I let them gift us with a couple of nights stay there in the first place was because I thought you might like it—having grown up in a swanky neighborhood in Dallas and all—and because I forgot to arrange for a honeymoon for us."

Surely that wasn't guilt she saw reflected in his gorgeous blue eyes. It wasn't as if she had planned anything for their wedding night, either. Or even stayed around to enjoy the spoils of the proffered luxury.

She re-capped the ice cream and put it away. "It's not as if we were getting married in the real sense."

Silence fell.

"I'm pretty sure it was legal."

The thought of being tied to him forever made her catch her breath. "You know what I mean."

Mischief sparkled in his smile. "I do…"

"Then…?"

He shrugged his broad shoulders nonchalantly, but there was nothing detached about the look on his face. He sauntered closer. All hot, hungering male. His come-hither grin widened. "Seems like hot sex is one of the perks of saying our I Do's."

It certainly should have been.

Hiding her disappointment about how her recent pregnancy-induced aversion to shrimp had eliminated that on their wedding night, Sage shrugged. "Oh, well…" Maybe those days were about over with, anyway. With the sexual mystique gone and her waistband expanding…

He sobered. "So how are you feeling? Overall?" His gaze drifted over her kindly. "Any more nausea?"

Aware she was close to falling for him in the traditional way they had both wholeheartedly agreed to avoid, she squared her shoulders and said, "No."

Satisfaction radiated from him. "That's good."

Silence fell between them. The kind they usually filled with hot kisses, and more. But not when she had a headful of goop.

Figuring maybe she should at least offer to whip something up for him, before sending him on his way, she said, "Did you have dinner?"

"On the road. You?"

She nodded. "One of the requirements of pregnancy. You have to eat regularly." She amended self-consciously, "Something more than ice cream."

He nodded, understanding a craving was a craving. Particularly in her state.

Suddenly aware she wasn't in a hurry for him to leave after all, she paused. "You mind if I jump in the shower and rinse this goop out of my hair?"

His gaze drifting over her lazily, he shook his head. "Mind if I make myself at home while you do?"

Trying not to read too much into her suddenly racing heart, Sage murmured, "Go right ahead."

NICK WAITED UNTIL Sage had disappeared into the bedroom, then eased back out into the hall outside her apartment. There, he had everything he needed.

And it was a good thing, too. Since his bride was every bit as overwrought and worked up as he had figured she would be. She might tell him everything that had happened to them the last week or so was no big deal. But he knew it was.

What lay ahead of them was even more important, he thought, as he quickly made preparations. Which was why he had to take the reins in their relationship. At least for now...

He had just finished setting up when the door to the bedroom eased open once again.

Sage paused in the portal, blinking as her eyes adjusted to the candlelight. She finished running the towel over her wet hair, then let it fall limply to her side. "What are you doing?"

"You really don't know?"

For a moment, she looked as if she might hazard a guess, then pulled back and said warily, "Haven't a clue. So suppose you tell me, cowboy."

Once again, all the barriers around her heart were up.

He smiled. Her feistiness didn't deter him in the slightest. He ambled toward her, slowly and purposefully, then said, "I'm here to claim our wedding night."

Chapter Six

Sage jerked in a quavering breath. "That's really funny, Nick."

He let his gaze drift over her, taking in her sweet lusciousness from head to toe. She had put on a pair of soft gray leggings that ended just below her knee, leaving her shapely calves, trim ankles and delicate bare feet in full view.

An oversize blue denim shirt fell past her hips, disguising the budding changes in her lithe body nearly as well as the chef's coats she wore to work.

Her hair was still damp, falling in silky dark gold waves to her shoulders. Her lips bare and soft and mutinous.

He could hardly blame her for acting guarded. Spiriting her off for an unexpected honeymoon, which he stupidly hadn't planned, and then ditching her early the next morning to go to work had *not* been cool. Regret lashed through him. She'd tried to hide it but he'd seen the stricken look on her face. The forty-eight hours since the wedding had been a total and utter disaster. And he had no one to blame but himself.

But he had every intention of making it up to her. Right here. Right now.

He spread his arms wide on either side of him, forcing himself to be the gentleman he had been raised to be. "I'm not joking."

Her chin lifted indignantly. "Well, you should be. Because need I remind you?" The color in her cheeks deepened. "We aren't really joined in the state of holy matrimony, at least not in the usual sense."

"Which ought to make this all the more entertaining. Since—" he let his gaze drop to the nipples pearling beneath the soft fabric of her shirt "—we won't be constrained in any way."

"Except one." She walked over to examine the bottles of sparkling apple juice and water, on ice. She opened the fruit beverage and poured some into two of the champagne flutes he had provided. Walking over to where he stood, she handed him one. "I'm really not in the mood for any faux romance."

Wow, she was prickly tonight. Pregnancy hormones? Or pissed-off woman? Luckily, he was braced for both.

"Neither am I." He took their empty glasses and set them aside. "Still, I think it's important to get back in the saddle as soon as possible, and replace some not-so-great recollections with new and improved memories."

Wrapping one arm around her waist, he hauled her closer. Dropped his head and kissed her neck.

He murmured, "Perhaps some mood music?" Reaching for his phone, he scrolled down the playlist. Found the song that made her laugh every time.

The sound of Marvin Gaye's "Let's Get It On" filled her apartment. She groaned and dropped her head comically to the width of his shoulder. "No."

He searched some more. Hit the more upbeat "Lookin' For A Good Time" by Lady Antebellum.

She chuckled in defiance and glided away from him.

Propping both her fists on her luscious hips, she said, "I'm sensing a theme here."

So was he. He two-stepped closer. "And the answer is…?"

Wary stubbornness glittered in her eyes. "No…"

Of course that was her answer.

Because she knew if she relented, let the guard around her heart down just a little bit, what would happen. What he had long hoped would happen.

Determined to end the unexpected tension that had sprung up between them, he hit Stop and then Play again.

The first strains of John Legend's "All Of Me" floated in the air. The beauty of the music brought forth tears. Something he had seen before. And remembered.

She caught her breath, and he knew he had hit a home run. Wordlessly, he closed the distance between them and took her hand.

The beautiful music surrounded them. She melted against him as he wrapped her in his arms again.

He'd half expected her to keep holding back on him, out of both residual anger and disappointment, and her ever-present need to keep them from getting too close. But she wreathed her arms around his neck, opened her mouth to the plundering pressure of his and let her body soften against him.

He'd thought the times they had made love, up to now, had been sweet and incredibly satisfying. But those times were nothing compared to this, as he tangled his hands in the silky dampness of her hair, and she kissed him back with a wildness beyond his most erotic dreams.

She trembled in his arms, and he moved his lips to the lobe of her ear, the hollow beneath. "Let's go to bed," she whispered.

Not an invitation he would refuse. Keeping his arms

around her, he danced her slowly backward into her bedroom, kissing her all the while. Her lips were ravenous against his, and for once she didn't try to hide how she felt. Nor, as she moaned softly and curled up against him even more, did he.

And yet, he thought, as the sweet urgency of desire swept through him, making love with Sage had never been a simple thing. Much as she might wish it so. By her own admission, she had kept the need in her locked tightly away. And put her own romantic yearnings aside, too.

Their marriage was supposed to be a means to an end, nothing more.

Yet, as he felt the soft surrender of her body pressed against the rock-hard demand of his, their union felt all too real.

And that gave him pause.

He had been raised to never take advantage. To put his cards on the table and let the chips fall where they may. And he knew he had deceived her about the depth of his feelings from the very first. He lifted his head and looked into her eyes. "You know I never meant to mislead you," he began.

She bent her head and concentrated on unbuttoning his shirt. "You haven't."

He tried again as she opened the fabric and ran her hands lovingly over his chest. "Our relationship—"

Her hands dropped to his belt. "Is exactly the way we want it to be," she purred.

SAGE DIDN'T UNDERSTAND what was with Nick tonight. All she did know was that she did not want to see the guilt and regret suddenly reflected in his deep blue eyes. Any more than she wanted to feel the conflict that had been rising up within herself since the moment they had said their I Do's.

It was as if everything had changed. And nothing had changed. And she wanted things that were both frustratingly undefined, and just out of reach. She wanted them to be together for more than just business. Or their baby. She wanted them to love each other with wild romantic abandon, and make a commitment to each other that lasted the rest of their lives.

But this was not what they had promised each other. And she did not want Nick to feel as trapped—by her demands—as Terrence had.

So she returned to the things that bound her and Nick together from the very first. Friendship and fun, explosive sex.

Slipping back into the role of carefree vixen, she eased his pants away from his waist. Or tried. He caught her palms in his, and held them out on either side of her. Eyes gleaming, he decreed, "Ladies first."

She both hated and loved it when he took charge like this. It made her feel far too vulnerable, too ripe for his taking. Her breath caught in her throat. "Nick…"

Too late, he had let go of her wrists and was already busy divesting her of her shirt and stretchy cotton bra. With her breasts bared to his view, he looked his fill, in a way that had her nipples crowning all the more.

Sexy grin widening, he stripped her leggings and panties down her legs. Knowing by now it was hopeless to fight it—she would be battling against the flame of desire that could only be doused one way—she rested her hands on his shoulders and stepped out of both.

Then, instead of rising, he wrapped his arms around her and pressed his lips against her for the most thrilling of kisses. Her knees buckled, just like that. He chuckled in masculine satisfaction, and kept right on exploring. While she held on for dear life, he dallied provocatively, finding her every sweet spot with ease. Trying not to think about what the newly proprietary nature of his love-making meant, or how close she was to surrendering every ounce of her fast-dwindling independence, Sage drew in a shuddering breath. Aware she felt both ravished and cherished. "Nick…" *My Lord, Nick!*

Eyes glimmering with mischief, he gave her body one last affectionate squeeze, then rose. "You're probably right," he teased, "we do need to get more comfortable."

Not exactly where she'd been going. But…who was she to quibble with success? Or near success, anyway?

Her insides melting like butter on a hot stove, Sage watched him hungrily. Tall frame radiating barely leashed energy, Nick dispensed with his own clothes, shifted her backward and stretched out next to her on the bed.

"Now…where were we?" he growled.

As if he didn't know.

"I think it's my turn, cowboy." In an effort to regain control, she attempted to flip him onto his back. To no avail. It was like budging a boulder. A very hard, very big boulder of intense male energy.

She swallowed as right before her eyes, his arousal grew. "If you're ready…"

"We're taking our time." A decision, not a request.

Sage gulped. What was going on with him? "Nick." She tried again to assert some control.

"Sage." He mimicked her low tone perfectly.

Her throat went even drier.

"Let me."

Two words. One indomitable, hungry, oh-so-male

look. And she opened herself up to him like a flower in the spring.

He kissed his way up and down, over every inch of her body.

When she came apart in his hands way too soon, he held her until the aftershocks stopped, then moved upward, as resolute and unstoppable as the general of a conquering army. Palms beneath her hips, he rested his weight on his knees. Lifting her gently, brought her up flush against him.

Just that quickly, she found heaven.

She could feel his body pulsing with the same fierce, unquenchable need she had seen etched on his face, as they began to kiss again. Passionately at first. Then more gently. She arched against him in abject surrender. His mouth moved inexorably over hers, tempting, teasing, claiming. She moaned as he gave another kiss, more soulful and exciting than the last. And then, without warning, he brought her closer still, and they were one. Moving toward a single goal, climbing ever higher. Until unable to help herself, she soared over the edge, this time taking him with her.

Long moments passed, as they continued to hold each other in replete silence. Shuddering. The sound of their ragged breaths still meshing, their heartbeats slowing in unison.

Nick ducked his head. As if savoring the way she felt in his arms. The essence that was just her.

Sage found herself doing the same.

She didn't want to want her new "husband" with this incredible, soul-deep intensity.

But she did.

She didn't want to need him in ways that she sensed could never be undone.

And yet she did. And that could be the ruin of them both.

FOR LONG MOMENTS AFTER, Nick and Sage snuggled close. As always, neither of them was in any hurry to move away and Sage felt the surge of contentment and inner peace that only he could give.

Yet as he stroked her hair and continued to hold her close, Sage could sense something was on Nick's mind. Finally, he asked, "Feeling better?"

Sage cuddled closer, the heat from his body still engulfing hers. She knew the effective businessman in Nick liked to identify and address problems before they snowballed out of control, but it unnerved her when he put the same skill set to their relationship. Hoping to avoid any serious talk, she lifted her head. Smiling. Shrugged. "What makes you think I wasn't okay when you got here?"

He held her eyes. "Call it 'husbandly' intuition."

His candid words unsettled her in a way she didn't expect. Maybe because, deep down, a part of her wished that they did have the potential for something more than friendship. Passion. And now a child they would share, and love, together.

But the boundaries in their relationship had been established early on. And there was no sense in fixing what wasn't broken, she told herself sternly. Especially now, with so much at stake.

She eased from the bed, and to keep them from making love again when she was suddenly feeling so vulnerable, began to dress. "I admit I've been feeling a little depressed."

His dark brow furrowed. "How come?"

Sage turned away from his searching gaze, as always leery of revealing too much. "Luisa calls it the post-wedding blues. She says it's the way all brides feel after the big day and the honeymoon, or in our case, the one that wasn't."

Reluctantly, Nick followed her lead. Putting the charcoal gray suit pants and shirt on.

Tenderness and understanding radiated in his gaze. "Listen, I know the past forty-eight hours haven't been the best, but I promise, I'll make it up to you."

She bet he would. The way he just had. In bed.

As for the rest...

His business was going to have to continue to take priority for him. As would the oft-unexpected rigors of her pregnancy for her.

Which meant, married or not, she couldn't let herself expect more—from either of them.

She walked into the other room of her apartment and headed for the small but well-outfitted kitchen.

He took a seat at the island and watched her move about the work area, doing what she always did when she was stressed-out. Cook.

Nick rested his forearms on the granite countertop. "So what is the cure for the post-wedding blues supposed to be?" he asked, in that low, husky voice that melted her from the inside out.

Sage got out a loaf of sourdough, ham, eggs, spinach, onion, gruyere and cream. "Settling into normal married life, realizing that it can be even more wonderful and magical than the ceremony."

He considered Luisa's theory dubiously. "Sounds like a lot of pressure on day-to-day living."

Which they both knew, especially when they weren't together, could be as dull as watching paint dry.

"My thoughts exactly. The thing is, I don't know how we're going to avoid dealing with it," she said as she layered torn pieces of bread into the bottom of a glass casserole, than began to whisk the eggs and cream. "There's already so much expectation for us to personify the ultimate in passionate romance because we're…"

"Newlyweds?"

Sage added butter to the skillet on the stove and began to sauté the onion, Once again aware how cozy and right this all felt. "It was one thing to be expecting a baby together. I mean, no one knew for a few months but the two of us and my doctor. But still, there is a happiness associated with the coming birth of a child that we both felt."

"And still feel," he murmured affectionately.

Sage forced herself to continue. "And it wasn't hard, because until we announced our happy news to everyone last week, we weren't having to *pretend* the way we are now."

He gave her a quizzical look.

"About the marriage and everything," she explained self-consciously, putting the rest of Nick's favorite breakfast strata together. "The real reason behind us getting hitched in the first place."

"We're both consenting adults, Sage. I don't think anyone thinks it was a shotgun wedding, even if you are pregnant."

He paused to let his words sink in. "Whether our families approved or disapproved, we could easily have not gotten married, if that was what we wanted. People who know us—know how strong-willed and independent we both are—know that getting hitched was a *choice* we both made."

Except there hadn't been a choice, Sage thought unhappily, given the way MR and the other venture partners had insisted.

"And we made that choice happily," he finished emphatically.

She could see that was true—for him.

For her, the decision was a lot more complex, in retrospect.

Which was really ironic. She'd gone from being the woman who once "unfairly pressured and ensnared" her ex into a long-term relationship—at least to hear Terrence tell it—to the one in the equation who felt imprisoned by circumstances way beyond her control. At least if she wanted the man in her life to be as happy and fulfilled as he could be...

Aware Nick still didn't seem to get what the problem was, she covered the prepared dish and put it into her refrigerator to bake first thing the next morning.

She brought the dirty dishes over to the sink, as did he, and began putting them in her dishwasher. "I don't want the intimate details of our decision to wed to be common knowledge." As she straightened, her hip bumped against his.

Swallowing, Sage lifted her chin and continued, "It's bad enough Hope and Garrett know." Although both her brother and sister-in-law had been sworn to secrecy, and she knew they would keep their confidence, it still rankled, realizing she and Nick had been pushed into this.

It had seemed so simple and easy at the time.

Now...

Was Everett Keller, right?

Was she on the verge of losing her best friend? And all because she'd made Nick her husband?

His mood as quietly accepting as hers was troubled and pensive, Nick went to her fridge. He helped himself to the Texas beer and a container of spicy mixed nuts, which she kept on hand just for him. While he lounged against the counter, enjoying his own snack, she got out a spoon and the carton of Rocky Road she had been work-ing on when he arrived.

Together, they moved to the sofa. As she settled cross-legged next to him, Nick continued to study her curiously. "I agree that we're entitled to our privacy."

Good, Sage thought, relieved.

"So…why do you think we have to do anything be-sides make it clear to people that we're good together and really happy about the coming baby? Why do you think we have to *pretend* anything?"

Sage spooned up some of the frozen treat with more than her usual concentration. "I guess we don't, but…" With effort, she looked up into his imploring blue gaze. "We live here. And I at least will still be working here full-time, even if you're gone a lot." Sage paused, and as her next thought occured, she confirmed, "You *will* be gone a lot…?"

Nick nodded.

"For the next three or four months," he affirmed matter-of-factly. "After that, I plan to be here a lot more than I'm gone."

Relief filtered through her. Again, she pushed it aside.

She didn't *need* a husband. She didn't *need* Nick. She could want him, and cherish him, and she did…but she had to be as okay without him as she was with him if she wanted to be happy from here on out.

His mood turning sultry, he ran a hand lazily down her thigh to her knee. "So what else is on your mind?"

He was going to get wind of the rumors she'd begun to hear that morning, whether she told him or not. So maybe it was better it came from her. "Until I moved to town you were a very eligible bachelor."

"Not sure I'd put it that way."

"Trust me. Women were lined up to go out with you."

She mugged at him playfully. "You were just too busy plotting your next business maneuvers to notice."

"And your point is…?"

She fought a flush with only partial success.

"Now that the news about our pregnancy has spread, I feel like everyone is looking at me, wondering if I trapped you into this situation via my pregnancy."

"You didn't."

"I know that. And you know that…" But now that the rings were on their fingers, it was open season on the speculation.

Nick set his beer aside. "Do you want me to take out an ad in the *Laramie Bugle* newspaper? It could say something like 'I, Nick Monroe, impregnated this woman with all my heart and soul…'"

She couldn't help but laugh.

Shaking her head, she leaned forward to elbow him lightly in the side. "I don't think that's going to solve our problem, cowboy. But you're right, it would definitely end the 'ensnared' storyline."

He squinted comically. "I could tell everyone *you* proposed joint parenthood to *me*."

Which was, unlikely as it might seem to outsiders, the truth. Sage put a hand to her temple to mime warding off a migraine. "Ah. Please don't. My mother would hang both of us out to dry!"

And after arguing bitterly with her mom the previous summer about her proposed plans to have a baby on her own, Sage did not want to do that.

Her mom was the only parent she had left.

She did not want to disappoint Lucille, even if it meant concealing the truth. Something she also did not want to do. Which left her between a rock and a hard place.

Nick reflected, "We could just amp up the whole newlywed routine. Appear ecstatically happy." He removed the pillow behind her and lifted her over onto his lap. "Make out in public and stuff."

Back to sex again. As always. Not that she usually minded. She set her ice cream aside and wreathed her arms about his neck. "You're a dangerous distraction, you know that, cowboy?"

He flashed a wicked smile, kissing her temple, her cheek, her lips, then said softly, seductively, "There's a lot more where that came from, darlin'." Excitement roared through her as he found her mouth, indulging in a long, hot kiss that quickly had passion sweeping through her.

Long moments later, they drew apart. Sage had only to look into his eyes and feel his hardness to know he wanted to table this discussion indefinitely and take her to bed again. And while she fully intended to take him up on that invitation eventually, she put a staying hand to his chest. "As tempted as I am, let's get serious here for a moment, Nick. How are we going to quash the scrutiny? 'Cause with you gone, I really don't want to be pitied." *Or feel reason to be.*

Nick lifted her wrist to his lips, and kissed the inside of it. "You could travel *with* me some of the time."

And depend on him even more than she already was? Ignoring the new tingling the kiss engendered, her own growing need, Sage shook her head. "I did that once."

He tensed but his expression did not change. "With Terrence?"

Finding she suddenly needed her physical space, Sage got up to put her ice cream away again.

"I spent seven years following my ex from job to job. I lived in Silicon Valley, San Francisco, Portland and Seattle. And quit job after job, all to be with him."

He lifted his shoulder in a hapless manner. "You were engaged, weren't you?"

"In the end. Because I really wanted to be, and we both felt obligated, because of all the time we had spent together, to make it work. Only to find out…" Her voice caught. Suddenly, she was glad they had the width of the living area between them.

"What?" he asked gently.

Maybe she needed to tell someone. Maybe then the unbearable humiliation would end. She began wiping down the counters. "That Terrence had never really wanted to be with me that long, after all," she said in a low, choked voice. "He just hadn't known how to break up with me. So he'd let himself remain trapped in the convenience of it all."

A muscle ticked in Nick's jaw, the way it did over any injustice that was done to her. His gaze seemed fixed on her hand. "Sounds like a real jackass," he growled.

Sage sighed and put the spray bottle of cleaner and paper towels away. "I was at fault, too. I saw the signs, but I just kept thinking if I could somehow keep the romance in our relationship alive, I could make it all work in the end." She paced the length of her kitchen restlessly. "We'd have this grandiose happily-ever-after life that I know now doesn't even exist."

Slowly, deliberately, Nick got to his feet. "What do you mean 'it doesn't exist'?" he asked casually.

He neared her, his big body filling up the space.

Sage lounged against the counter. "You know, the fairy tale most of the girls I grew up with…believed in." She had to tip her head back to see his handsome face. "You grow up thinking that you'll go to college and get the perfect job, and find the perfect mate, and get married and have kids and live happily-ever-after." She shook her head sadly. "But nothing is ever perfect, Nick. Not even close. Because in reality, I have to create my own happiness. Not make it contingent on anyone else."

Even you, Nick.

NICK KNEW WHEN he was in trouble, and he was in big trouble now. Calling on every ounce of persuasiveness he possessed, he moved toward Sage and said, "Look. I understand your disappointment over a failed relationship. I felt it too when both my engagements went bust."

The tension in her shoulders eased slightly. "You never said why exactly that happened."

There wasn't much to tell. "I did the same things, both times. Pushed too hard, too fast, to achieve the kind of happiness you say doesn't exist."

Her lower lip forming a delicious pout, Sage folded her arms in front of her. "It doesn't. At least not outside of fairy tales."

In no hurry to engage her in further argument, he studied her for a good long time. "Well, let's just say after losing both my folks in an accident at age ten, I wished like hell that it had, back then. So I could have the complete family life I lost." And in fact, he still wished it.

Only now the fantasy had a particular woman starring in it, and she was standing right in front of him, her heart suddenly on her sleeve.

"Oh, Nick…"

Figuring if she had heard this much, she might as well know the rest, he looked her in the eye and said, "It was foolish to try to take a simple infatuation and turn it into more. But the fallout made me slow down. Temper my expectations just a little bit."

"Which is when you met me."

He couldn't help but grin at the feisty memory. "Who

also had 'tempered' expectations." To the point, she'd told him flat-out she wasn't going to "date" anybody. Hence, he'd detoured onto the just-friends zone.

"See?" She smiled despite herself. "We're a match made in practicality."

Nick just wished that was all he wanted from Sage. But even being her lover and husband in name only wasn't enough.

Her soft hands lifted in a conciliatory manner. "And now we're having a baby together."

He ignored the erratic intake of her breath and the clear definition of her breasts beneath the loose shirt. "That's right, sweetheart. We've got an awful lot to be thankful for right now. So, maybe we should just use that—" *and our increasingly intense feelings* "—to keep the gossip at bay."

She blushed prettily and kept her eyes on his. "What do you mean?"

He moved toward her and planted a hand on the counter on either side of her. "I suggest we give everyone as much truth as they can handle. And let 'em know how happy we are, and have been for months now, even before the whole baby and marriage thing. Tell them we didn't say anything to anyone because we didn't want to risk jinxing the best thing that had ever happened to either of us." Which was, for him at least, the complete and honest truth.

"You think that will work?"

Loving the warmth and softness of her, as much as the yearning in her lovely eyes, he said, "I think relaxing about everything is always worth a try." Unable to keep himself from touching her, he plucked a stray curl from her cheek and tucked it behind her ear. "And speaking of upcoming events…" He paused to let his gaze rove her upturned face. "Didn't you tell me you had an ultra-sound coming up?"

Sage radiated with excitement. "When I hit the five-month mark."

"Still want me to be there?" Thus far, she hadn't seen the need to invite him to any of the appointments. Except that one.

Sage merely nodded. Then she bit her lip, looking almost afraid to hope for too much again. "Do you think it will be possible?"

He wrapped both his arms around her and hugged her close. For a moment appreciating the soft surrender of her body against his. "I'll be certain that it is," he told her gruffly. "Wild horses couldn't keep me away."

Chapter Seven

Sage sat next to Nick when he talked with his four siblings at Triple Canyon Ranch late afternoon the following day. As his wife, he'd explained, she was now expected to attend the Monroe family business meetings, whenever possible. "Although I originally hoped to expand Monroe's Western Wear into a multi-location corporation, with venture capital money, it's become clear that is just not going to work. So, the new business is going to be an entirely new and separate entity."

"Your new business partners were okay with that?" Gavin asked his brother with his usual directness.

Nick slanted Sage a self-assured look, then turned back to his sibs. "They understand all five of us inherited equal shares in Monroe's Western Wear and the ranch. And that although I draw a salary for running the store, the profits are already split five ways, and will continue to be. There simply wouldn't be enough return on their investment for them to be involved, as is."

Nick passed out the papers the lawyers had prepared. "Hence their decision to go with something entirely new, while still utilizing my knowledge of the Western-wear clothing business."

Pretty, blonde Erin scanned hers. "How much money are you putting in?"

"None," Nick reported succinctly. "In exchange for my work in getting the projected six new stores up and running, I'll get a 49 percent share, while Metro Equity Partners will retain 51 percent ownership. The eventual profits will be split the same way."

"You're okay, not being in control?" Bess asked with a heartfelt concern Sage shared.

Nick shrugged haphazardly. "I've got a son or daughter on the way."

Which wasn't exactly an answer to the question, Sage thought. Not sure that aspect of the deal was going to be as easy for Nick as he seemed to think now.

"Not to mention a wife to support," Gavin added.

As all eyes turned to her, Sage flushed. She had tried to tell Nick that she did not belong at what was in essence a private Monroe family meeting. That she could sign the necessary legal papers at another time, but he had insisted. Even though his two older married siblings hadn't brought their spouses.

"Nick and I agreed before we married not to share our assets," she explained, looking everyone in the eye, "so I won't be laying claim to any profits he reaps. And vice versa."

Her pronouncement was met with a mixture of understanding and approval from the two younger unmarried siblings, and skepticism from the two older married ones.

As if sensing she felt more ill at ease than ever, Nick reached over and squeezed Sage's hand. "The bottom line is I'd prefer not to empty my bank accounts for a start-up. I'm happy just to put in my time and effort and have all my travel expenses paid. If it's the success everyone expects it to be, I'll be making plenty of money in the long run."

Sage hoped so. She knew how much financial success meant to Nick. As much as it had to her dad.

"I'm guessing you'll have to travel a lot?" Bridgett asked.

"In the beginning," Nick confirmed.

"What about the ranch?" Gavin queried.

"I've already hired a married couple to take care of the property and the horses."

Erin's glance drifted to Sage's tummy and the baby she was carrying. "Where is Sage going to stay?" she asked with maternal concern.

As all eyes turned to her, Sage spoke up. "In my apartment, in town."

"When I'm gone," Nick said, with a clarifying look aimed her way. "When I'm here, she'll be with me, at the ranch."

This was news to Sage. But again, was something everyone would expect in a happily-married couple. So she nodded agreeably, even though she and Nick hadn't actually come to a consensus. Generally, they just did whatever they felt like at that moment.

Silence fell.

"So what do you need from us?" Erin asked.

"Your signatures on the partnership agreement, stating your rights extend only to the ranch and the flagship business, not any new ventures. Sage, as my wife, you will need to sign, too."

The pages were passed around.

Signatures gained.

Nick collected the papers, and collated them into one neat stack. He looked at his siblings. The dining room was so silent you could have heard a pin drop.

To Sage's acute disappointment, there was none of the

happiness or congratulations she would have expected. And Nick needed.

"Okay," he said shortly, unable to completely conceal his hurt. "Obviously, you all have reservations. Let's hear 'em."

"Life is really short," Bess, a nurse who worked with rehabbing vets said. "Are you sure you want to spend it on the road?"

Her twin, Bridgett, an NICU nurse at the hospital, predicted worriedly, "You're not going to want to leave that little baby, once he or she is born."

Erin, the oldest, who had run the store and the ranch herself a number of years, said, "I know it can look easy, from the outside, but running the store in Laramie is pretty time-consuming on its own."

Which was why, everyone knew, Erin'd had to step down and just focus on her young family and custom boot-making business.

Gavin, an ER physician, added, "The money sounds great."

"But…?" Nick prodded with a frown.

Gavin shrugged. "I just can't see you kowtowing to someone else's business plan."

Wow. Sage blinked. Before she knew it she was on her feet, her hands flat on the table in front of her. Aware she had never felt more protective of anyone in her life, she chastened all four of Nick's siblings with one sweeping glance. "I think this is an incredible opportunity for your brother. He's worked hard and is deserving of your congratulations." *Not your private reservations!*

"You're absolutely right," a chastened Erin swiftly agreed. With an apologetic smile, she rose and walked around to embrace Nick warmly. "Sorry, little brother."

His three sibs followed suit, offering handshakes and

hugs, too. The meeting over, everyone left to return to their own obligations. Nick lingered on the front porch of the ranch house beside her. The evening stretched out ahead, breezy and cool. He turned, his emotions locked up tight as a drum. "You didn't have to jump to my defense like that."

Yes, Nick, I did.

I couldn't bear to see you so momentarily beaten down.

"Hey," she teased softly, wary of coming on too strong for fear of pushing him away or further adding to his misery. "What are wives for?"

Sadness tinged his smile. "You've got a point," he returned.

He'd been there for her, so many times. It was her time to be there for him. Sage stretched out her hand. "Come on, cowboy." She winked. "I've got just the thing."

AN HOUR LATER, they had taken his pickup to the highest point on the Triple Canyon ranch. "I can't say I'm surprised your idea involved an intimate dinner for just the two of us, given how much you like to cook. But can I say how glad I am it involved the kind of food only you can prepare?"

Sage grinned.

"And the back of a pickup truck." He gestured magnanimously. "And the view of the three canyons at sunset." For which his family's ranch had been named.

Sage leaned against the back of the cab, her legs stretched out on the thick layer of blankets lining the truck bed. "I've never seen anything this beautiful," she murmured as they polished off the last of the steak tacos. "How come you never brought me up here to see the sunset before now?"

He put their dishes into the basket. Tucked her into the curve of his arm and kissed her temple, teasing, "'Cause I figured you'd fall in love with the land and not me."

Love.

She just wished their emotions were that intense.

"Sorry." He mugged. "Bad joke."

Sage drew a deep breath, and looked out at the purple-and-pink streaks against the backdrop of the slowly darkening Texas sky. "No offense taken."

The only reason she was even the tiniest bit upset was that this whole adventure was so damn romantic. To the point that the promise of never bringing anything as problematic as love into their relationship was getting difficult.

Nick moved far enough away to see her face, and took her hand. "Something's off."

"I was just thinking about your sibs' reaction," she fibbed.

Nick took her hand in his. "From their point of view, they probably have a right to be worried. I am the baby of the family, you know. After my folks died when I was ten, everyone had a part in raising me."

She liked it when he confided in her like this. It made her feel closer to him. "Let me guess. You were the rebel."

He squeezed her fingers companionably. "More like a wannabe Warren Buffet."

Trying not to think how handsome he was, or how much she always seemed to want to make love to him, Sage sighed. "Back to money. Lots of it." Just like her father.

"And success. But I have to admit, the money would have been great to have back then. We struggled, trying to hold on to everything after Mom and Dad died. Sold all the cattle. Went through what savings there was, trying to pay the taxes on the land, and still fell woefully behind." He released a breath. "If it hadn't been for Mac Wheeler coming to town, putting the wind energy turbines on our land, we might have lost everything, including the store, despite all our best efforts to the contrary."

"But now you don't need the money. The ranch pays for itself and the store is doing a booming business."

His brows took on a determined slant. "I do need more of a challenge. This could be it."

"Could be?"

He frowned. "There are some things I didn't tell my sibs."

Curious, Sage tensed. "Like what?"

"They're planning to make the stores a lot more high-end and seat them only in urban areas."

Sage blinked in surprise. "I thought the idea was to link them in some way to the success of the original mercantile. Have you as spokesperson."

"They are still going to do that, although in a roundabout way. Meanwhile, the Monroe name and four generations of expertise selling Western wear will help them promote the venture."

So he was being used. Willingly, albeit, but...she had to ask, "You think you're going to be happy with the finished product?"

As darkness descended, Nick turned on the camping lantern. It filled the bed of the truck with a soft, intimate light. Whatever demons he had had been put to rest. "MR has assured me that I'll still have a great deal of input."

Sage looked on the bright side. She might not believe in his new partners, but she definitely believed in him. She smiled. "So then it can't help but be a success. 'Cause I'm sure you'll handle whatever comes your way."

"Like I 'handle' you?" Nick teased, shifting her over onto his lap.

Sage settled intimately against him. "Ooh, sexy, cowboy!"

Nick stroked a hand through her hair, down her spine. "Ever made love in the bed of a pickup truck?" he asked huskily.

Sage shook her head, ready for the pleasurable diversion he offered. "Can't say that I have." She pressed her lips lightly to his. "Is that about to change?"

"Let's see." Nick rubbed his thumb across her lower lip. Slanted his head. "First we'd have to kiss…"

Sage opened her mouth to the insistent pressure of his, savoring the heat and taste of him. "Very nice so far…" she decreed.

Nick smiled and reached for the buttons on her blouse. "Then we'd have to get a little closer still."

She quivered as he undid the clasp on her bra, and bared her to his touch. "Also nice," she whispered, unfastening his shirt, too.

"And touch." He shifted her over her onto her side, and stretched his frame alongside hers. Facing each other, they kissed and stroked until his sinewy chest tautened and her nipples pearled and her blood ran hot and heavy through her veins.

Needing more, they kicked off their jeans.

Sage lay on her back, knees raised. "And become one…"

Resting his weight on his forearms, he slid home. Sage caught her breath, the force of her own desire driving her to wild abandon. Excitement racing through her, she ran her hands through his hair and held his head. "Good thing we fit together so nicely…" she murmured, her breath coming raggedly.

Nick paused, searching her face. "And in every other

way," he affirmed in the rough sexy voice she loved. He flashed her a deliberately provocative grin, and took her mouth again in a long, hot, tempestuous kiss. As desire swept through her, he settled on top of her, his weight as welcoming as a blanket on a cold winter's night.

Savoring the intimacy, the emotional connection that only seemed to get more intense every time they were together, she wrapped her limbs around him, pulling him deeper still.

"Nick," she whispered. *Oh, Nick...*

He went deep. And slow.

She arched up to meet him.

And then all was lost in the swirling passion, their climaxes merging as irrevocably as they were beginning to merge their lives.

"COME WITH ME TODAY," Nick encouraged the following morning, after another bout of sweet and sensual lovemaking—in the shower at her apartment this time—had left her body humming.

Aware she didn't want to leave him, either, Sage shrugged on a thick terry-cloth robe. "Back to Dallas?"

He wrapped his arms around her and pressed a kiss into her hair. "We could work in some honeymooning in the evenings."

The days, Sage already knew, would be spent working on the new business venture. She slipped away from him and picked up a wide-toothed comb. "I bet MR would really like that."

Frowning, Nick finished drying his body. "You're not jealous of her, are you?"

Only in the sense that the exec was suddenly spending a lot more time with Nick than she was, Sage thought, as she began detangling her wet hair.

Yet the question reminded her of what Everett had told her as he escorted her to the town car at the hotel, indicating she was not gaining a husband, but instead losing her best friend.

She met his glance in the bathroom mirror. "Should I be?"

Grinning, Nick replied, "What do you think?"

Sage shrugged. *If I knew, I wouldn't have asked.*

Nick turned her gently around to face him. Planting his hands on the counter, on either side of her, he leaned over her and delivered the kind of long, soulful kiss that left her breathless and trembling and in no doubt of how much he desired her.

When he finally came up for air, he paused, his gaze drifting over her. As always, seeing far more of her inner vulnerability than she wanted him to see. "What's really bothering you?"

Something stupid someone else said.

But not about to become the kind of clinging woman who needed constant reassurance from her man, Sage pushed aside her niggling uncertainty.

"Sage?" Nick pressed, his gaze narrowing in concern. "Come on. Level with me. What is it?"

Actually, Sage thought, there were about a hundred little things. She picked one. "I know it's silly, but…I'm a little nervous about the sonogram."

A lot could go wrong with a pregnancy, and although hers was progressing nicely to date, according to her obstetrician, Sage had also read enough online to know that could change at any time.

Complications cropped up. Perfectly laid plans were forced to be abandoned…

Nick laced a reassuring arm about her shoulders and pulled her in close to his side. "I'm still planning to be there. Two fifteen, right? A week from Friday? Your OB's office?"

"Dr. Johnson. Right."

"It'll be amazing," he predicted with a grin as wide as all of Texas.

"I know." *I hope. I wish...*

"Our first glimpse of our new baby!"

Thus far. Although she had heard her baby's heartbeat, loud and strong, at her last appointment, Sage had yet to feel him or her kick. She had been told it could happen at any time in the fourth or fifth month, and several times she'd almost thought she felt something, only to wonder if she had only imagined it.

She drew a breath and tried to get a grip on her soaring emotions. This was all hormones, she promised herself, nothing more.

"Speaking of our little one, I need to purchase a crib and a changing table." She paused at Nick's inscrutable expression. Frustrated to find she still couldn't read him anywhere near as well as he could read her, she said, "I wasn't sure if you wanted to go with me for that...or...?"

He paused, looking completely at a loss. Why, she wasn't sure.

Sage moved away. "Actually, never mind. I think it might be better if I went with Molly and Adelaide, since they have already outfitted nurseries, and know exactly what to buy."

Nick's relief was palpable. "I'd be happy to put it together," he volunteered happily, looking around. "The larger question is, where are you going to put it?" he asked. Her apartment consisted of two large rooms and a bath.

Sage grimaced. "Not sure yet."

Nick tugged on jeans and a shirt. "Do you want to go

ahead and get two cribs then? One for your place? One for mine? I'll reimburse you, of course."

Yep, they were definitely back to the business side of their relationship. Trying not to feel disappointed—this was what they had agreed upon after all—Sage smiled. "Do you want them both to be identical or different?"

He deferred again. "You decide."

O-kay. Wishing he were a little more enthusiastic about setting up an infant space, Sage watched Nick's glance cut to the clock. Suppressing her frustration, she asked, "Need to get a move on?"

He drew her toward him and dropped a tender kiss on her forehead. "Unfortunately, yes." He smoothed the hair from her face. "But—" he paused to kiss her one last time "—I'll be back before you know it."

Chapter Eight

"You're in a hurry."

Sage put the closed sign on the door. "Shows, huh?"

Luisa nodded. "Nick coming home tonight?"

Finally! "He should be in at about eight this evening," Sage reported. Which gave her roughly four hours...

"Cooking dinner for him?"

Shutting down the coffee machines, Sage feigned nonchalance. "I told him I'd throw something together."

"Which means...?"

"Man food. Steak. Baked potatoes. Salad. And of course the quintessential apple pie."

"Just make sure you don't get too tired to give your man a proper welcome home." Luisa winked.

Sage rolled her eyes, although she was expecting their reconnection to light up the sky with fireworks.

"Seriously, I'll finish up here. You go get ready for your man."

Sage hugged Luisa. "Thanks." She whipped off the barista apron, let herself into the hallway adjacent to the back alley and headed up the staircase. Inside, her apartment sparkled from a recent cleaning. Her fridge was filled with fresh ingredients. And she was brimming with excitement.

Nick had been gone ten days, most of which had been

spent on the road with MR and Everett, meeting with potential suppliers. She hadn't heard from him yet today, but he had called or texted or emailed every other day. Just to see how she and their baby were doing. It had felt good, being connected to him that way, even if their communications had sometimes been rushed. So she was eager to catch up completely.

And that excitement stayed with her as 8:00 p.m. came and went. Still with no word from Nick. No call or email or text. Which really began to worry her. It wasn't like him not to let her know he was going to be late. Never mind *this* late.

Finally, around eleven, she texted his sister Bridgett. Her phone rang a few seconds later. "What's going on?" Bridgett asked.

Sage explained. "But, now that I'm saying all this out loud, I feel like I'm being silly, contemplating worst-case scenarios."

"I'm sure Nick's on his way," Bridgett soothed. "Otherwise, he would have let you know. Maybe he's out of cell phone range. You know there are a lot of dead spots between here and Dallas. But listen, if you want me to call all the other sibs..."

"No. You're right." Sage shook off her increasing sense of dread. "I'm letting my imagination get away from me. He'll be home before I know it."

AT MIDNIGHT, SAGE went to sleep. Sometime after that, her cell phone rang.

It was MR Rhodes, requesting a FaceTime chat with her.

Heart jumping with anxiety, Sage switched on the bedside lamp, drew the covers over her chest and accepted.

MR appeared on screen, dressed in her usual elegant business attire. "Sage. Sorry to wake you."

Sage shoved the hair out of her eyes, glad she had worn a demure sleep shirt to bed. "Is everything all right?"

"We're just behind schedule. Which is why Nick asked us to get in touch with you."

That was weird. Embarrassing or not, she had to ask. "Is there some reason he couldn't contact me himself?"

"He's still meeting with the Santa Fe artisans who are trying to get their goods in our new venue. They've been coming to the hotel all day to show us what they can provide exclusively for us, and since Nick is the expert on Western wear, he's riding point on the discussions."

Made sense. Sort of.

MR smiled. "Anyway, he wanted you to have his flight information for tomorrow morning. Everett, can you please give it to Sage?"

The phone changed hands.

Everett appeared on screen. There was a second's pause, as he took Sage in, with what might have been a flash of remorse or indecision in his expression. Then he glanced down at the tablet in his other hand and read out the airline and flight number. "Departs at 6:07 in the morning, and arrives in Dallas at 9:20."

"Thank you, Everett. Text that information to Sage."

Everett disappeared from view.

MR came back into the picture. "So even if there is traffic Nick should easily be able to make your ultrasound appointment tomorrow afternoon. He wants you to know that. So…you're good?" MR said crisply.

Sage forced a smile. "I am. Thanks for calling."

They ended the call.

As much as Sage wanted to, she couldn't go back to sleep for several hours after that. Her mind kept replaying the warning Everett had given her the morning after she married Nick, the way he hadn't quite wanted to look her in the eye during the FaceTime chat.

Did he know something she should?

Or was it just the way the venture capital/start-up business worked that had MR's assistant so sure trouble was brewing for her and Nick?

One thing was for certain. You couldn't build any kind of successful relationship if you rarely interacted with the other person. And, Sage thought miserably as she wrapped her arms tightly around her pillow and sought comfort where she could, that was certainly becoming true for her and Nick.

"How many texts have you had this morning?" Luisa asked, sliding another tray of apple Danish into the oven to bake.

Sage spread a thin layer of jalapeño cream cheese on some tortillas. "Thirty-two." *In five hours.*

Luisa cast a look toward the front of the shop. Just after eleven, the lunch crowd had yet to come in. Satisfied the part-time counter help could handle things for the moment, she turned back to give Sage a concerned look, "All from Nick?"

Sage layered thin slices of mesquite-smoked chicken overtop, then added slices of avocado, heirloom tomato and red onion. "Every last one."

Luisa added cooled brownies to a display case tray. "Bad news?"

"He's still fogged in, in Santa Fe." Which meant he would miss the ultrasound.

"Can you reschedule?"

Sage rolled the sandwiches, sliced them in half, then covered them with plastic wrap. "Not without twenty-four hours advance notice," she admitted glumly. "Besides, I really want to take a look myself and see the baby is okay."

"Still not kicking?"

"Not that I can tell." Sage fell silent. And though she knew from her readings that it could be as long as the twenty-fifth week before a first-time mother felt her baby kick, she still worried. The anatomy scan would show them definitively that everything was okay.

So Sage went to her obstetrician's office alone, at the appointed time. Signed in, turned off her phone and drank the water they gave her. Twenty minutes later, Sage's bladder was uncomfortably full, and she was reclining on the exam table, a pillow beneath her head.

Dr. Johnson walked in. "Ready?"

Feeling unbearably excited and incredibly sad to be experiencing this moment without Nick at her side, Sage nodded. She turned her head toward the black-and-white monitor while the gel was smeared over her midriff.

"Here we go," the obstetrician said, picking up the transducer wand and moving it over her belly. And suddenly, there, on screen, were lots of wavy, fluid lines. And through the shifting movement, the poignantly beautiful image of their baby's head.

She stared at the screen in wonder and relief. It was all just so incredible…

"Here's the baby's heart."

She could actually *see* it beating, steady and strong.

"And legs and arms…" Which were indeed, Sage noted, *moving*, even if she couldn't yet feel the motion inside her.

"Everything is looking good," Dr. Johnson said with satisfaction as the last of the measurements were taken and recorded. He turned to her, kind as ever. "Do you want to know the sex?"

Bad enough Nick was missing this. To miss that, too…? Sage felt a burst of generosity that far surpassed her anger and disappointment with her baby's daddy. "No," she said firmly. "We'll wait until the baby is born to find that out."

AFTER A DAY of travel hell, and many unanswered phone calls to Sage, Nick got in close to 9:00 p.m. Friday evening. He found Sage right where he expected she would be. In her bistro kitchen, working on the next day's offerings.

In white capris and a loose-fitting dark blue shirt that covered her baby bump, her wheat-gold hair upswept in a clip, she looked gorgeous, and ticked off as all get-out.

Though she had to have heard him use his key and come in through the service entrance off the back hall, she ignored him steadily.

He couldn't blame her. He was wracked with guilt at not being able to keep his promise, forcing her to go to their baby's ultrasound alone. He felt even sadder about missing such an important milestone in their relationship and their child's life. This was more than just a missed opportunity, it was a moment in time he could not get back. And he would make up for that.

But first, he had to make amends.

He set his bag down. "Sorry can't begin to cover it, I know."

She stared him down, growing even more flushed. "Do tell."

Damn, she was ticked off. "I'm as frustrated as you are."

She arched an elegant brow. "Somehow I doubt that."

"Okay." He girded himself for the worst. "Let me have it."

Even icier. "I'd rather not."

Nick tried again but could not quite keep the exasperation from his voice. "I sent you a message."

Sage set her rolling pin down with a clatter. "Yeah, that was great. Having MR and Everett call me at *midnight*. Four hours after you were supposed to be here for dinner. Really nice, Nick. *Really nice.*"

She thought he had stood her up without a word? "What are you talking about?" Nick moved closer. "We knew we weren't getting out of there last night *at noon* yesterday."

Sage wiped her hands with a towel. "Well, that's news to me."

With a weariness that went soul deep, he said, "I thought you had been called."

She tilted her head to one side and kept her eyes on his. "You really couldn't have done it yourself?"

Hell, yes, he wished he could have. But this was what happened, he was beginning to realize, when you gave up control of a business venture.

He shoved a hand through his hair. "If you had any idea how crazy it was the last ten days. How many vendors I've met, and spaces I've toured. Meetings I've been in."

All for you, Sage. And our baby...

Because if it hadn't been for the two of them, he would have said to hell with it all and pulled out of this malfated venture long ago.

But he couldn't.

Not if he wanted to give Sage the kind of ultraluxurious life she had grown up with.

She wanted to believe in him, in them. He could see that. She just wasn't sure she should.

Shoulders stiff, she finally looked right at him and allowed in a low, strangled voice, "I know you've been busy, Nick." Her chest heaved with each breath. "I've been busy, too." Amber eyes glistening with tears, she swallowed and pushed on. "I don't fault you for working hard," she murmured, clearly distraught. "But I still would have made it to our baby's ultrasound." She reached into her pocket and pulled out a black-and-white photo. Their fingers brushed as she thrust it at him. "I still would have moved heaven and earth not to have missed this."

He stared down at the ghostly image of a baby. Their baby. The miracle of it nearly slammed him to his knees. For a moment, he could barely breathe, let alone speak. "Is that the head…the legs…?" he asked, his heart bursting with love.

Affirming proudly, Sage pointed. "Arms…"

Of their kid! *Their kid!* "Sucking a thumb?"

Sage allowed in a low, proud voice, "The nurse said that happens in utero all the time. And if they pacify themselves that way while they are inside their mommy's tummy, they usually do it as soon as they get out of their mommy's body, too."

How cute was that going to be? Amazing.

They stared at the image some more in wonderment. Moving nearer, he wrapped one arm around Sage. Finally, he pulled himself together enough to ask, "Do we know if it's a girl or boy?"

Still holding herself stiffly, Sage shook her head. "I told Dr. Johnson I didn't want to know yet. I thought you should at least be there for that."

He turned her so she had no choice but to face him. He felt like a kid who was telling a teacher the dog ate his homework, but she needed to understand just the same. "I tried like hell to be here."

"I know," Sage said wearily, recalling the gist of the

many text messages he had sent her that morning. "But the Santa Fe airport was fogged in this morning, and all the flights were delayed until almost noon, and the one you were supposed to be on eventually got canceled due to mechanical problems."

It had been the Murphy's Law of Travel day for him. He held her by the shoulders, needing, wanting to understand her. "So why did you stop responding to me? Why didn't you pick up when I called?"

She slipped out of his light grasp.

Her lower lip slid out in the delicious pout he knew so well and could never stop wanting to kiss. "Because I was too angry, and I shouldn't have been. And I knew that," she confessed in a thick voice. "And I didn't want to say something I would regret."

He studied her sullen expression, figuring she'd earned the right to have her say. And truth to tell, he wanted to hear it all. So they wouldn't find themselves in this place again.

She stomped closer, arms akimbo. "We made a deal, Nick, when this all started. That you could be around as much or as little as you chose, and I would never ever put any kind of pressure or expectation on you, or leave you feeling trapped in any way. Yet I was doing just that." She shook her head in silent remonstration, then aimed a thumb at the center of her chest. "And that made me angry at myself. And then add in a few pregnancy hormones…" Her voice broke. She waved a dismissing hand. "I needed to calm down."

He studied her upturned face. "And have you?"

For a moment he thought she was going to lie, then she sighed. "I'm working on it."

"Then you're ahead of me," he returned with grim

honesty, moving closer. "Because I'm probably going to be upset with myself for a while."

Her eyes widened in surprise.

Obviously, she hadn't expected a mea culpa from him.

"I should have left yesterday as planned. MR and Everett could have stayed and handled the remaining business meetings. But I didn't. And I missed something I never should have missed." He put his hands on her shoulders and waited for her gaze to meet his. "I'm really sorry, darlin'," he said in a low, tortured tone. "More sorry than you'll ever know."

She could see that.

Her anger evaporated.

"I'm sorry, too." Sage ran her hands through her hair. "I didn't think things through. I should have explained the situation and rescheduled. Since there was no medical emergency precipitating the ultrasound, we could have just waited until you were available. So—" she drew in a ragged breath "—I'm at fault here, too."

Nick helped Sage put the baked goods into the walk-in for the next day. "So, truce…?" he said as they walked out, shutting the door behind them.

Sage nodded, taking off her apron. "Truce."

"Only one problem with that," Nick said.

Sage's delicate brow furrowed in confusion. "What?"

"This is no way to make up after our first fight as a married couple."

"Actually," Sage corrected, flashing an impish smile, "it's our first real fight."

"You're right. It is." And he never wanted to have one like this again. So…

He stepped forward, tucked one hand beneath her knees and swung her up into his arms. She let out a low squeal and held on to his shoulders.

FREE Merchandise is 'in the Cards' for you!

Dear Reader,

We're giving away FREE MERCHANDISE!

Seriously, we'd like to reward you for reading this novel by giving you **FREE MERCHANDISE** worth over **$20** retail. And no purchase is necessary!

You see the Jack of Hearts sticker above? Paste that sticker in the box on the Free Merchandise Voucher inside. Return the Voucher today... and we'll send you Free Merchandise!

Thanks again for reading one of our novels—and enjoy your Free Merchandise with our compliments!

Pam Powers

Pam Powers

P.S. Look inside to see what Free Merchandise is **"in the cards"** for you!

We'd

like to send you two free books like the one you are enjoying now. Your two books have a combined cover price of over $10 retail, but they are yours to keep absolutely FREE! We'll even send you 2 wonderful surprise gifts. You can't lose!

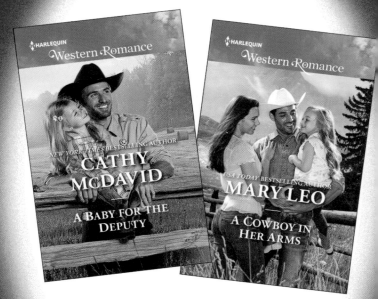

REMEMBER: Your Free Merchandise, consisting of **2 Free Books** and **2 Free Gifts**, is worth over $20 retail! No purchase is necessary, so please send for your Free Merchandise today.

Get TWO FREE GIFTS!

We'll also send you 2 wonderful FREE GIFTS (worth about $10 retail), in addition to your 2 Free books!

Visit us at:
www.ReaderService.com

"Well, this is getting interesting."

He returned her grin. "You think so?" He bent to kiss her cheek. "Just wait."

He headed out the service door of the bakery and carried her easily up the back stairs to her apartment. Set her down long enough for her to unlock the door, then picked her right back up again.

She gave him a mock-stern look. "You know I may be pregnant, but I can still walk."

Sensing they were at a turning point in their relationship, he cradled her in his arms. "But should you have to?"

She chuckled, clearly as turned on as she was exasperated.

"Seriously." He looked down at her adoringly. "During those long, long hours when I was waiting to get home to you, it occurred to me I never carried you over the threshold."

She hitched in a breath.

"And now seems like the perfect time." He walked through the front door, through the living area and into the bedroom, before setting her gently down next to her bed...

Sage wanted to continue to keep things simple with Nick.

But the moment his hands lifted her shirt and moved higher, his thumbs running over the tender crests, she felt herself begin to lose herself in him all over again.

She hadn't allowed herself to want anything as much as she wanted him in a long time. Hadn't allowed herself to hope that they could have anything close to a fairy tale.

Wise or not, she wanted to lose herself in the bliss, the intimacy only he could bring. She wanted the explosion of heat and hunger his kiss wrought. Overwhelmed by the pleasurable sensations, she returned his kiss with everything she had.

His need and yearning mirrored hers.

She surrendered against him one moment.

He took total control the next.

Until they dropped down on the bed, and she arched against him, the need in her an incessant ache. And still it wasn't enough for either of them, as she ran her hands over hard muscle and smooth skin. He was absolutely beautiful. So beautiful, she couldn't take her eyes from his sculpted pecs and abs, and lower still…

Yes, he wanted her.

Oh my, he wanted her.

He rolled her onto her side, so they were facing each other. And still they kissed, until her heart filled and her entire body throbbed with searing heat.

Flush with victory, he slid a hand between her legs, making her blossom, sending her quickly to the brink. Knowing this was no time to be selfish, she guided him inside her. Together, they soared. Found. Conquered. And came slowly, inevitably, back down.

And Sage knew all was right between them once again.

Chapter Nine

"Look, I'm sorry," MR said, the following morning, over FaceTime with Nick. "I thought it would be better to wait and call Sage when we had the flight change nailed down. And that took a while."

Nick supposed that was true. The storms that had hit Santa Fe the previous day had wreaked havoc throughout the West Coast, leaving a lot of people stranded, scrambling to get home.

"Luckily, I was finally able to reach a VP friend at the airlines and he was able to manage it for us. But—" MR paused, her expression penitent "—the next time we need to get a message to her, I'll make sure Everett does it right away, even if we don't yet have everything worked out."

"That won't be necessary," Nick said. "From now on, any communications between me and Sage will be handled by me."

MR frowned and moved on tersely. "When can we expect you here?"

"I won't be returning to Dallas until Monday afternoon."

Another pause, while MR stared him down.

"Nick, with a Father's Day weekend opening, we really don't have 48 hours to waste. The lease for the space in Dallas has to be signed *today*."

"So, sign it," Nick returned implacably. "Metro Equity Partners has 51 percent control. You don't need me to finalize that."

Nick looked up to see Sage standing in the doorway of his office. He repeated, "I've got to go."

"One sec." MR snapped her fingers. Everett appeared in the background, computer tablet in hand. "We at least need to schedule a daily call."

No. They didn't. "Whatever it is, we can do it Monday afternoon." He ended the call and turned off his phone.

Sage lingered in the doorway. "Am I interrupting?"

He shook his head, wondering if she had any idea at all how much he missed her when they were apart, or how glad he was to be with her now. "Never."

He moved away from his desk, brought her into his arms and kissed her. She surrendered against him, basking in the fierce tenderness flowing between them.

When they finally drew apart, he paused to take her in. Instead of the white chef's coat he expected to see her in, she was wearing a pretty green shirt over her jeans, and the comfy sneakers she now usually chose over her boots. "I thought you were going to work this morning."

Sage grinned. "I decided to take the day off since you're here. Unless—" she paused, glancing with trepidation at his phone "—you're leaving again?"

Nick shook his head. "Not until Monday."

Her amber eyes glowed with the same happiness and contentment he felt. "So you're footloose and fancy-free?"

Steps sounded in the hall. Nick's twin sisters, Bridgett and Bess, appeared in the doorway.

"Not exactly," they said.

"A BABY SHOWER?" Sage echoed in surprise.

"We knew Nick was coming in for the ultrasound yesterday," Bess said. "So we planned it for this morning. It's going to be held at your mom's ranch. Everyone from both families is going to be there."

Sage wasn't sure whether to well up with joy or groan in distress. The happiness she and Nick shared was so fragile, she wasn't sure it could hold up under intense familial scrutiny.

"It starts in forty-five minutes, so get a move on," Bridgett advised. "And bring the photo!"

As Sage had feared, no sooner had she and Nick arrived at the Circle H and were passing around the very first photo of their baby than the questions began. "So, what did you think of the ultrasound?" Nick's older brother, Gavin, asked.

"It was amazing," Sage said.

Erin looked at Nick, curious.

Never one to dance around a problem, Nick grabbed the bull by the horns. "I missed it due to flight delays," he said. The room fell silent.

Sage's mother was the first to recover. "That's a shame," she said sympathetically.

Nick took Sage's hand. "It's the last thing of importance I'm going to miss," he vowed protectively. "From now on, I plan to be at every obstetrics appointment with your daughter."

Now, it was Sage's turn to be surprised. "That's really not necessary," she said. Especially since at most of them all she did was step on a scale, pee in a cup and have her abdomen palpitated.

"Yes," Nick said firmly, "it is."

At that, everyone smiled.

And although she had promised herself she would not allow herself to rely on Nick too much, Sage couldn't help but feel really happy, too.

Her ebullience lasted throughout the party. Nick remained content in a way she had never really seen him, too. They were both still smiling as they arrived back at her apartment.

"Is that the last of it?" Sage asked, several trips from the vehicle later, as Nick walked in, his arms laden with baby gifts.

"Yep." He carried the bassinet over to the corner of her living room. "You want this here, too?"

Sage nodded. Between this and the wedding gifts, much of which was still in boxes, awaiting a decision— her place or his—it was beginning to feel more like a storage facility than a home.

Starting to feel overwhelmed, she knotted her hands in front of her and stared at the mess. "I thought I was going to have plenty of room to have our baby here. Now... Nick, we don't even have a crib or a changing table yet!"

His brow furrowed. "I thought you were going shopping for baby furniture for both our places."

"I special ordered identical sets. They won't be delivered for another few weeks, but when they do arrive..."

Nick caught her wrist. "We'll figure it out."

Ignoring the tingling in her arm, she slid out of his light grasp. Moving away from him, she put her hand to her lower back, rubbed restlessly. "When?" She walked a short distance away. "The baby will be here in another four months!"

A long thoughtful pause followed. "Which gives us plenty of time. What's the matter?" Nick cocked his head. "Did you hurt yourself carrying those packages up the stairs?"

"No." Sage stopped pacing.

The truth was, he'd barely let her carry anything.

He came closer. "Then why are you rubbing your lower back?"

Sage jerked in a deep, enervating breath. Realizing what she had been doing, she dropped her hand. "It's been bothering me since I hit the three-month mark."

"Did you tell your obstetrician?"

Sage waved off his concern. "Yes, and Dr. Johnson said, that pelvic and or lumbar discomfort is common in pregnancy. It's due to the growing uterus and hormonal changes."

He gave her a telling look. "What are you supposed to do to alleviate it?"

"Stretching exercises. Walking. Pelvic tilts. Prenatal yoga."

His gaze caressed her face. "What about massages? Do those help?"

"I'm sure they do," Sage retorted, "but I can't exactly do that to myself."

He grinned at her wry tone. "Which is why you have me here."

The heat within her intensified, but it was the kind of heat that usually presaged their lovemaking. "You're kidding."

"Nope." He tucked his hand in hers. "Luckily, these days, there's a how-to video for everything." Ten minutes later, Nick had watched enough to feel educated. "All right, first thing we have to do is get you to lie on the floor, and we'll turn you slightly on your side, and put one pillow beneath your neck and head, the other between your knees."

Sage knelt on the thick quilt they'd spread out in her living room. "You sure you want to do this?" She didn't know why but she was suddenly feeling very shy.

The grooves on either side of his lips deepened. "Hush, woman."

"Hush, woman?" What had gotten into him!

With gentle hands, he guided her into position. "You can't relax if you're talking."

Her back to him, Sage struggled to get comfortable. She tossed him a quelling look over her shoulder. "When did you get so bossy?"

"The day I realized you—and our baby—needed me."

He was so right about that. The funny thing was he looked like he needed them as much as they did him.

Sage was still trying to wrap her mind around that as Nick knelt on the floor behind her.

"Okay, we're going to start on one side of the neck." With an unclenched fist, he massaged his way magically down to her hips, on one side of her spine, then slowly worked his way back up again. His touch was so purposeful and heavenly it was all she could do not to groan in ecstasy. "Now we're going to try both sides," he soothed.

As he worked his way downward, this time she did moan out loud. He chuckled. "Feel good?"

Her muscles were warm and fluid. Sage sighed. "You have no idea…"

"Good. We'll keep doing it until you're…"

And then, out of nowhere, Sage realized, there it was. A flutter, a movement, a… "Nick!" Sage gasped.

He jumped back slightly. "Did I hurt you?"

"Give me your hand," she whispered. Staying very still otherwise, she beckoned him to comply. He reached over her. Sage captured his palm and settled it slightly above her navel.

His dark brow furrowed in confusion. "You want me to massage you there?"

Oh, no, please don't make me laugh, not now…

"Shh!" She stayed still, waited, and then there it was again. The slightest flutter, then nothing, then a kick.

Nick went very still, too. Amazement shimmered in his deep blue eyes. "Was that…?"

"Our baby is kicking!" Sage said, tears of sheer joy starting to flow. She turned her head slightly to look at him. Saw he was overcome with emotion, too.

"Was that the first time?" Nick asked in a rusty-sounding voice.

Sage nodded, her heart so full it was practically bursting. "I guess Little One was just waiting for you to be here, too."

"STILL NOTHING?" NICK asked in obvious disappointment, several hours later.

Sage shook her head.

They'd gone to the ranch to check on the property and had dinner outside on the porch. Now, replete and relaxed, they sat together in the chain-hung swing and watched the sun go down. Sage curved her hand over her blossoming belly. "I guess our little one has decided once again to do things on his or her own time."

Nick rested his open palm next to hers. He leaned down to kiss her neck, then murmured playfully in her ear, "What do you think we're having? Girl or boy?"

Sage shut her eyes, quivering, as he kissed her again, this time on the sensitive spot just behind her ear. "No idea."

He shifted her masterfully onto his lap. "Which do you want?"

Aware it really didn't matter, Sage wrapped her arms around his broad shoulders and nestled against him. She kissed the nape of his neck, too. "I'll be happy either way," she confessed softly.

He turned his head toward hers. "Me, too."

Once again, a contented silence brought them together. Their lips met. And when they started kissing, it was impossible to stop. All coherent thought fled and a lightning bolt of desire swept through her. This, she thought, was what it felt like when it was right.

This was what she had always wanted…

Nick hadn't intended to make love to Sage out on the swing, but with the moon shining brightly down at them from a starlit sky it seemed foolish to waste such a perfect setting. Especially when he wanted her so much.

She shuddered as his hands swept over her. Before they knew it, they were naked from the waist down. Coming together once again, with Sage astride him. Kissing. And when he lifted her, the sensation of filling her left them both quaking and breathless.

He couldn't get enough of her softness and warmth. While he held her right where he wanted her, right where he wanted her to be, their lovemaking turning from pure passion to a deep all-encompassing need.

He held her close, closer, savoring every delicate caress, each sweet surrender. Every tremble. Every kiss. Connection. As they met each other stroke for stroke, her newly voluptuous body cradled him tenderly. Until finally, they surrendered to the blazing heat, the need, the intimacy.

To their mutual pleasure, the aftershocks were as potent as their lovemaking had been. And though this was the only time Nick ever felt Sage was all his, he knew, for now, it would not only have to be enough. It would be.

SAGE WOKE TO an empty bed. Nick was downstairs in the living room, clad in a T-shirt and jeans, laptop open on his lap, cell phone beside him. "Why are you up so early?" She ambled closer, wearing socks and one of his big shirts. "I thought we agreed to sleep in this morning."

They'd been planning to eat a leisurely brunch she cooked especially for him, then tour the ranch by jeep, checking out the property.

He set his laptop on the coffee table in front of him. "I didn't mean to wake you."

Not really the point. Sage folded her legs beneath her and cuddled up next to him. He looked so serious and so stressed. "What's wrong?"

His lips twisted unhappily. "I noticed last night before bed the voice mail box on my phone was full, and it looked as if I'd received even more emails, so I figured I'd better check."

"I gather there's some sort of emergency?"

Nick draped his arm along the back of the sofa and drew her against his side. Leaning over, he pressed a kiss in her hair. "MR and Everett were updating me on the partner meetings yesterday."

She turned toward him, appreciating how ruggedly handsome he looked in the early morning light streaming in through the blinds. "Were you supposed to be there?"

A terse nod.

Then he had skipped them, for her.

Sage wasn't sure whether to feel elated about that, or guilty. From the looks of it, he felt conflicted, too. Happy to be here, with her, worried about not being there, with them.

Nick rubbed his fingers through the mussed ends of her hair. "They were all playing golf yesterday morning…and then had a working lunch afterward at one of the partner's homes." He exhaled. "A lot of key decisions were made."

"Such as…?"

"The new name of the store." He retrieved his laptop and situated it so she could see the screen.

Sage blinked in surprise at the logo. "Upscale Outfitters?"

"It was either that or City Cowboy. Of the two that market-tested the best among their target customer, the former won."

Sage turned so they were facing in the same direction, and her body was pressed right up against his. She rested her head on his shoulder, reveling in the brisk masculine scent of him. "What are they going to be selling?"

With a click of the mouse, he pulled up several more windows on the screen.

Sage paused thoughtfully. "I recognize some of the brands." They were the kind of thing she had worn, back in the day when growing up a very wealthy Dallas teenager. But…

"They're not exactly ranch gear."

Nick shut his laptop, and set it aside once again. "You're right. It's all for the elite. People who are making a fashion statement rather than going out to round up cattle." He rose, and made his way into the ranch house kitchen.

Sage stood and lounged against the counter. "How do you feel about that?"

He began making coffee—decaf, on account of her.

"Since they just signed a lease on a storefront in the Galleria mall, it's a good business decision." Nick went to the fridge and brought out the makings for breakfast. "No working rancher is going to go there to purchase their work clothes."

"For that, they would come to the original Monroe's Western Wear."

"Right." He layered bacon in a skillet, while Sage whisked half a dozen eggs. "What happens next?"

"MR has set up a meeting with the interior designer who's going to design the look and layout of the flagship store."

Sage put four slices of oatmeal bread in the toaster. "When does that happen?"

"Three o'clock this afternoon."

Which was certainly doable, if he canceled their plans and left before noon. Sage studied him. "Do you want to be there?"

A conflicted expression crossed his handsome face as he turned back to the stove to flip the sizzling meat. Finally, he said, "To tell you the truth, I'm not sure what difference it really makes. With 49 percent share, I'm being outvoted on everything. Whatever MR wants, the partners back. Period."

And MR and Nick were not thinking the same way.

"Still...you must have some ability to sway things."

He dipped his head, acknowledging quietly, "Sometimes. When I'm there."

Instead of in Laramie, with her.

As much as she wanted to continue spending time together, she also knew how important this was to him.

Sage added a touch of cream, salt and pepper, and poured the eggs into the pan. "Then you've got to go to that meeting," she said quietly. *Or end up looking back in regret at what might have been.*

He shook his head, determined now. "This is our day together, Sage."

"And we'll have plenty more of them," she argued.

He went still.

"You won't have another day to shape the feel and mood of the flagship store. So have breakfast here, like we planned. Then shower and go. Get it done." She rose on tiptoe and kissed him. "You can call me tonight and tell me all about it."

He wrapped his arms around her and pulled her against him, for another longer, deeper kiss. "You really are the perfect woman for me."

Sage was certainly trying to be.

If only they loved each other, too, then life really would be perfect. But that wasn't part of their deal, she reminded herself, so she would be happy the way things were. And so, hopefully, would he.

Chapter Ten

"You're really leaving to go back to Laramie," MR said as Nick gathered up his things, a couple months later. "Again."

Nick zipped his laptop bag. "Sage has an appointment with her obstetrician."

"Routine appointment," MR clarified. "And there's still much to do to get ready for the grand opening next month."

He was well aware. It was also Mother's Day weekend. His and Sage's first. "That's five weeks away."

"And half the orders of merchandise have yet to arrive. Plus, we need to talk about the advance interviews you've been doing. Without our approval or consent."

Getting more than a little tired of the constant haranguing, Nick gave MR a long, level look. "You asked me to talk to every local TV station, newspaper and magazine, as well as the publications that cover the high-end Texas consumer."

"In June."

Nick exhaled. "I may not be available then," he explained patiently. "So I'm doing everything I can *in advance*."

MR scowled. Behind her, Everett looked up. Briefly,

the assistant regarded Nick with a mixture of surprise, respect and pity, before resuming his usual poker face.

MR looked at him as if he were a dollar short and a day late. "The publicity needs to herald the advent of Upscale Outfitters. And, hence, appear in the days *immediately leading up* to Father's Day weekend."

Nick exhaled. "I've explained my situation, MR. Everyone's been very accommodating in doing the preliminary interviews with me now about the Western-wear business, and the tour and photos of the new store a few days before they go to press in June. They also know that if unexpected events occur and I'm unavailable for that, you and/or Everett will be happy to show them around and provide them with any further information they need."

MR stalked closer. When she spoke again, it was in a much more conciliatory tone. "I appreciate your diligence, Nick, but Sage isn't due until July first."

Nick looped his computer briefcase over his shoulder. "That's an estimate. She could give birth before or after that day."

"Unless her doctor induces her." MR flashed a winning smile. "Then you would know exactly when the baby would arrive, and could plan for it."

Not sure what to say to that suggestion that would be remotely polite, a fuming Nick fell silent.

Seeming to realize she had crossed a line, MR shrugged. "Plenty of couples do it."

"For medical reasons, sure."

"For *convenience*," MR emphasized.

Not going to happen, not with our child. Hanging on to his temper with effort, Nick retorted curtly, "Our baby comes into the world when he or she is ready. And not a second before."

For a moment, MR seemed taken aback. Angry color appearing in her face, she gripped the pen in her hand. "You will be at the grand opening, regardless," she decreed.

Nick wasn't going to promise what he could not predict. So he merely said, instead, "I'll be back in Dallas on Monday." His heart already with Sage and the baby she carried, he headed out the door without a backward glance.

"So what do you think?" Sage asked her brother and sister-in-law the same morning.

Molly and Chance toured her apartment above the bistro, studying everything with a general contractor's and interior designer's eye.

"Is there any way I could make a separate nursery?" Without moving out to Nick's ranch? An act that still seemed like a risky endeavor, for so many reasons.

Chance measured the front room, a combination living, dining and eat-in kitchen, with a hidden laundry closet off the entryway. "This is fifteen feet by twenty."

Molly emerged from the bedroom. "It's fifteen by twenty, too. And the answer to your question, Sage, is yes." She pulled out a pad and pencil, and quickly sketched a rough design. "It would mean putting up a partial wall on either side of the divide with pocket doors."

"So I'd have room for a crib, changing table–dresser and rocker-glider in the new 'nursery.'"

Molly nodded. "And still maintain the walk-in closet and the bathroom on your side of the suite."

Sage put one hand on her lower back, which was aching as usual, and the other on her tummy, where the baby was attempting to ride a bucking bronc inside her. "Next question." She paced back and forth, wondering if she would ever get truly comfortable again. "Do we have time to get the construction done before the baby arrives?"

It hadn't been such a big deal before Nick had begun spending the night with her, whenever he was in Laramie. But now that he had, she wanted them to be able to have the privacy to make love comfortably, whenever he was in town. And just as important, she wanted their baby to have a cozy nursery to call his or her own, too.

Chance gave her a brotherly hug. To her joy, he fully understood her nesting. "Molly and I can have our crews knock it out in a day or two early next week."

Sage smiled in relief. "Great."

"Don't you have an OB appointment this afternoon?" Molly asked.

"Yup, at four thirty."

Chance squinted like the protective older brother he was. "Nick coming in?"

Sage reported happily, "He hasn't missed an appointment since the ultrasound."

"I'm glad," Molly said.

She glanced at her watch. "I better get back down to the bistro kitchen. Nick should be arriving any minute and wanted me to meet him there."

"How come?" Molly asked.

"Not sure. He just said it was important."

FIFTEEN MINUTES LATER, Nick had arrived. But Sage was not allowed to see him until he gave the signal. Which seemed to be taking forever to come, Sage thought, in mounting frustration. She wanted to throw herself into his arms, hug him close and give him one hell of a welcome-home kiss that would make them both breathless for more.

Instead, she was stuck in a corner of the bistro kitchen, as far away from the service entrance as possible, while her employees chuckled behind her.

"Eyes covered and closed?" Nick asked sternly.

"Yes," Sage replied, for what seemed like the fourth time.

"Okay." He was suddenly beside her, his arms around her, warm and encouraging, while she kept her hands over her eyes. "This way…" He guided her forward, then said triumphantly, "Open your eyes!"

Sage did.

In front of her was a tall beribboned chrome work stool on wheels, with a cushy black leather seat.

He grinned. "Happy Mother's Day!"

"It's…" She was speechless.

She had expected, if he gave her a gift, that it would be something like a necklace. Or flowers. Not…furniture.

On the other hand, it showed the depth of thought and concern she hadn't expected, either. And in that sense was incredibly sweet, as well as practical.

"It's completely ergonomic, with lumbar support, and adjusts dozens of ways. So you can cook in comfort, and won't have to be on your feet quite so much." He lifted a hand before she could interrupt. "I know. I know. We talked about this, and you have to do a lot of your prep work like chopping and dicing standing, but there are some tasks that can be done sitting, and if that helps you be more comfortable, or less physically stressed…" He nodded at her hand, which had, as it had so many times lately, unconsciously gone to her lower back.

"Thank you." Sage embraced him.

Exuding tenderness, he cuddled her close. "You like it?"

"So much that I have a feeling in a few weeks I'll be wondering how I ever lived without it!" Aware the more time went on, the more happily married she felt, she stepped back far enough to prop her hand on her hip and tease glibly, "My only question is where are you going to sit, cowboy?"

Grinning widely, he walked back out and came back rolling an identical fancy stool. "Problem solved."

She couldn't help but laugh, as around them her employees cheered his ingenuity, then exited to give the newlyweds coveted alone-time.

Sage went back into Nick's warm embrace. "You really do think ahead."

He lowered his lips to hers. "You have no idea, sweetheart." He started to kiss her, then drew back slightly to cup her tummy with the flat of his hand. The baby was kicking so hard her tummy was popping outward. "What is he or she doing in there?" he asked, astounded.

"I don't know. But it's been going on for about two days now…"

Sage's OB noticed the change, too. As soon as he had finished the exam, he ushered them into his office. Never a good sign. Sage and Nick took seats while he circled around his desk. "Is there a problem?" she asked anxiously.

"The baby is breech."

Nick clasped Sage's hand. "So if Little One were to be born right now…?"

"He or she would try to come out bottom first."

Which wouldn't work. Sage drew a quavering breath. Suddenly cold, she began to shiver. "What do we do?"

"Initially, we wait and see," Dr. Johnson told her encouragingly. "You still have plenty of room inside of you for the baby to turn on his or her own, and get back in the right position."

Nick held tight to Sage. "And if that doesn't happen?"

"Worst-case scenario, we may need to do a C-section and deliver the baby that way. But there are still seven weeks until the due date so it's way too premature for us to talk about that. Right now, we just need to wait and see."

Aware her first task as a mom was to stay calm, Sage sobered. "What can we do to precipitate that the baby gets back into position on his or her own?"

"There are some at-home turning methods to try but they aren't recommended for women who've had pelvic or back pain during their pregnancy, so I strongly caution you against those."

Briefly, Nick looked as disappointed as Sage felt. "Then there's nothing to be done?" he asked.

"Except relax, and let nature take its course," Dr. Johnson soothed.

Sage and Nick left the medical office, hand in hand. They walked wordlessly over to his pickup truck and climbed in. He started the truck, but made no move to drive anywhere just yet.

With cool air blowing out of the vents, he turned to her. His deep blue eyes were as worried as she felt, and tension etched the planes of his handsome face. "Are you okay?"

Sage caught her breath, trying not to cry. Finally, she swallowed. "Are you?"

He didn't answer, but then he didn't have to. She could see he was just as overcome with emotion as she was.

They sat for another moment in silence. "It's funny," Sage said finally. "I've been worried about how I'm going to manage in such a close space and where the baby is going to sleep when he or she does get here. Even though I knew problems could occur, I took for granted everything would go smoothly with the actual birth."

The irises of his eyes turned a darker blue. "Me, too."

Another silence, this one more fraught with emotion than the last. Finally, Nick cleared his throat. "Maybe it still will."

Sage drew a shaky breath. "What if it doesn't?"

"We have each other, sweetheart. And our baby has us." He flipped up the seat divider in his pickup truck, and moved across the space to take her in his strong arms. "Whatever happens," he promised her resolutely, "we're going to get through this."

NICK APPEARED IN his bedroom doorway, that evening, looking ruggedly sexy in a chambray shirt and jeans. "How is the relaxation going?"

Sage lounged against the pillows on his king-sized bed. She put down the novel he had insisted she read, in lieu of helping him with their dinner dishes. "How do you think?"

He handed her a bowl of praline ice cream—her newest craving—and settled beside her. "Is the baby kicking?"

Sage savored a spoonful of the rich delicious treat, then fed him one. "I feel movement every now and again but it's all up near my rib cage."

Nick stroked a tender hand over her baby bump. "Which means Little One is still positioned bottom first, near the birth canal."

"Probably." Sage sighed and ate some more ice cream.

Nick lifted the hem of her blouse and rested his head against her tummy.

Sage knew what Nick felt and heard. Absolutely nothing. "Where's our stunt-riding rodeo darlin' when we need him or her?" Nick asked, perplexed.

Sage sighed. "No kidding…" Of all the times for Little One to be content hanging out, doing absolutely nothing.

Nick pressed a soft kiss against her tummy, then sat up. "Seems to be sleeping now."

Sage gave Nick the last bite of ice cream, then set the bowl aside. Wondering what she had ever done without him, she informed him of their baby's schedule. "That's usually the case, early evening. It's in the middle of the night, when I'm trying to rest, Little One typically goes hog wild."

Nick's eyes twinkled. "Well, you know what they say about smart parents taking advantage of their kids' nap times…" He began to unbutton her blouse.

A thrill swept through her. When Nick kissed her, he made her feel cherished and adored, as if nothing mattered but the two of them, and what they felt now. With a soft exhalation of breath, she asked, "You really want to make love?" Earlier, neither of them had been in the mood.

His eyes sparkled with mischief. "I want to kiss. The making love can come later, or not. Depending."

She chuckled at his exaggerated sternness. "On…?"

He waggled his brows. "How relaxed you are…"

"Nick…" He only looked at her like that when he intended to give her an amazing climax. He only gathered her in his arms, the way he was now, when he wanted them to feel connected, body and soul.

Smiling, he let his eyes drift over her, then lowered his lips to hers. "Just kiss me, Sage."

So she did.

Once. And then again. And again...

Afterward, they clung together. Feeling like husband and wife. Bonded as only worried parents can be. Which made their coming together all the sweeter. And Sage was very glad she did not have to face this alone.

Chapter Eleven

"Is that better?" Nick asked his wife, two weeks later, as he adjusted the pillows and heating pad behind her.

Sage nodded, turning to make sure the heating pad against her lower back was set on the lowest setting. Satisfied, she settled back into the cushy nest he had made for her. "Oh, yeah…" She gave his hand a squeeze and sighed luxuriantly, leaning back to wiggle her toes. "I can feel myself beginning to relax already."

Aware she only seemed to get sexier the further into her pregnancy she got, he lifted her hand to his lips and rubbed his lips across her palm. "I can think of another way."

She turned their twined hands over, and bent to kiss the back of his wrist with sensual accuracy. "You already gave me a back massage."

His body stirred. Lower still, he felt himself hardening. "Another way…"

"We did that, too," she reminded him. When they had turned in, the night before, and awakened this morning.

As if he could forget how good she felt, wrapped in his arms, her body pliantly entwined with his. He met her smile indulgently. "So how is Little One today?"

Sage curved a hand protectively over her rounded tummy. "Sleeping, I think, after being up most of the night." Which, he knew, had become typical in her third trimester.

But with only five and a half weeks left before the due date, it was something she swore she could handle. He tucked a strand of hair behind her ear, then stretched out next to her on the queen-sized bed that never seemed quite big enough. "Is that why you were so restless?" he asked, wishing he could take on some of the discomfort of pregnancy for her.

She nodded, sweeping her hair into an untidy knot on the top of her head. "I'm sorry if my tossing and turning kept you awake."

He wouldn't trade his time with her and their child for anything. Being awake with her just made him more present. But knowing she still wanted and expected them to keep things easy and casual, he shrugged off her restlessness and only said, "Gives me a chance to cuddle with the two of you."

Sage moved her head to rest against his shoulder. "You're getting pretty good at that."

He chuckled. "Nice to know…" He lifted his arm, shifting his body to accommodate her already cozily ensconced form, until he had brought her all the way into the curve of his body, without moving her off the pillows and heating pad that brought relief to her aching lower back.

Sage caressed her delectably rounded tummy. "I just wish I knew how to communicate to Little One it's time to do another 180 degree turn."

Nick had been doing some reading while he was away. The more he learned about breech presentations, and pregnancy and birth in general, the more worried he became. He'd never known so many things could go so wrong. But he had also made it his business to learn what to do in case of an emergency.

Knowing a positive attitude couldn't do anything but help, whatever the outcome, Nick soothed calmly, "There's still time for it to happen naturally. In any case, we've got a great hospital, with doctors and nurses that are prepared to handle everything."

Deliberately, Sage shook off her fear. Smiled, and said, "So true. And in fact…" She chuckled softly as her brows knit together in surprise. "I think someone else very important wants to weigh in on this discussion." She took his hand and put it just beneath her breasts. Just that suddenly, he felt it, too. A kick or punch…then another…

"See, even Little One is saying we should follow the doc's advice and try to relax about everything, so…"

Sage put a hand behind her, and awkwardly scooted toward the opposite side of the bed. She threw her legs over the edge, as restless now as she had been ready to take it easy a few minutes ago. "I think the best thing we can do is to stay busy. Because…"

Knowing how difficult it could be for her to change positions, he rose and walked around to assist her to her feet.

"It seems as if the more active I am, the more active Little One is."

Her delicate fingers encircled his bicep as she steadied herself. Lifting her face to his, she said, "And, the more likely he or she is to turn…"

Belatedly, Nick realized they should have gone out to the ranch to sleep the night before. Sage would have had much more room to maneuver in his king-sized bed. He also knew, now that she was starting to get closer to delivering, that she wanted to stay in town, near the hospital, as much as possible, just in case. "Is this your way of saying you want to tag along while I do inventory at Monroe's?"

She beamed. "How'd you know?"

Because like me, when we do have the opportunity to be together, you seem to want to be together nonstop. And that, too, was something new. Before they'd married, they'd both cherished their alone time, too.

"You sure you shouldn't stay here and rest, while I go look at the sales results?" He knew there were some problem areas with the current stock of Western wear. Apparently, the sales staff didn't have the same feel for the projected marketability of items as he did. Hence, they wanted him to review the orders for summer. Make sure they were as on track as they should be.

But none of that was Sage's problem. Protecting herself and her baby was her first priority. And the two of them, were his. Sternly, he reminded, "After all, this is your only full day off, every week…" And only because The Cowgirl Chef was closed. "Maybe you should take advantage of the quiet and just lounge about while I work."

She wrinkled her nose. "I don't really feel like napping." She sashayed closer. "And since I don't think you'll have me climbing up on ladders to check the stock on the higher shelves…"

He caught her in his arms and spun her around. "Definitely not." He dipped her playfully, righted her slowly.

"Then, I think I'll be perfectly safe, tagging along with you and lending a hand. And—" she pirouetted as he spun her around one last time, and then rose on tiptoe, to kiss him slowly and leisurely "—let's not forget, spending time with my favorite guy, to boot."

THE WORDS ECHOED in Nick's head long after they were spoken. *Favorite guy.* The endearment had been said with affection, he ruminated as they showered and dressed, and walked the short distance to Monroe's. So why was it rankling?

Maybe because he had figured they'd be really and truly married by now. Able to confess how much they had come to mean to each other. Because unless he was wrong, and he admitted ruefully he had been wrong in the past when it came to matters of the heart, Sage was as head over heels for him as he was for her. And had been for a while now...

Mistaking the reason behind his concern, Sage asked as they reached Monroe's, "Are you really worried about how the store has been doing in your absence?"

Yes and no, Nick thought, as he punched in the security code and let them in the back way. "Actually, sales have been good overall, but then, they always are, given what we carry."

She waited while he swung the door wide and held it for her. "The essentials for every working rancher. Male or female."

"Right." He closed the door behind them and hit the lights. "We price merchandise fairly every day, so we don't do big sales."

Which meant business was reliably steady, all the time.

Sage stopped abruptly in the middle of the store. Stood, with her hands on her hips. "Do you know that man, standing on the sidewalk, peering in?" she asked.

Nick turned to the front windows and saw a trim, forty-something man with a long brown braid, and a stone-colored Resistol hat. His shirt and jeans were nothing out of the ordinary, but the handcrafted solid silver-and-gold belt buckle holding together his rich leather belt radiated pure artistry.

"Yes, I do," he answered in surprise, staring at the noted silversmith. Although what Ed Durango would be doing here, on a Sunday afternoon, no less, was a mystery. Curious, Nick went to let the Santa Fe businessman in.

"Glad I finally tracked you down." Ed shook Nick's hand.

Nick rocked back on his heels. "I wasn't aware you'd been looking for me."

Ed Durango frowned. "I left a dozen messages for you with Everett and MR. Never got a return call."

Not good. And not surprising, unfortunately, given MR's need to control every tiny little aspect of the launch.

Figuring he would deal with that later, however, Nick asked kindly, "What's the problem?"

Ed rubbed his jaw. "Maybe you can tell me," he countered grimly. "I don't understand why Upscale Outfitters sent back the entire order of custom belt buckles."

Inwardly, Nick reeled. "I didn't know we had."

"Well, you did. And now I'm not going to get paid."

Nick bit down on a string of swear words. Resolved to get the other side of the story before he acted, however, he said, "Can you give me a chance to make a call?"

Ed nodded.

Nick took his phone out of earshot, while Sage chatted up Ed. As usual, MR answered right away. He did not like what he heard. Taut with anger, he returned to the noted craftsman. "Apparently, some changes were made without my knowledge."

Ed frowned. "Can you do something about it?"

Reluctantly, Nick explained he only had a 49 percent share in the new business, and had apparently been outvoted on a matter he had not even known was up for discussion. "But I'll make some calls and do everything I can for you," he promised.

Sage lifted a hand, looking like the down-to-earth hedge-fund heiress she was. "I know a family who owns a chain of jewelry stores in Dallas," she said, looking from Nick to Ed Durango, and back again. "I know they're always looking for high-end gifts with a Western flair. Particularly with Father's Day coming up. Perhaps if I put in a word…?"

"I'd appreciate it," Ed said, handing over his business card. "I really can't afford this kind of a loss."

"THANKS FOR DOING THAT," Nick said, when the silversmith had left. "Ed and I go way back. I met him several years ago, when he came to see if I would carry his belt buckles in Monroe's. The quality is far superior to anything I've ever seen, but it was way too pricey for the average cowboy."

"I'm guessing several thousand per buckle."

"As a starting point, since they're all solid silver and hand-engraved, and accented with 14-carat gold. Anyway, that's exactly the kind of item Upscale Outfitters should be carrying, so when we met with him in Santa Fe we placed a very large order. Enough to carry his company for the year."

Sage shook her head in sympathy, her heart going out to Nick. "And now it's been canceled. Without your knowledge. For heaven's sake, why?"

"MR and the partners decided the store was too Southwestern, so they called in upscale buyers from LA and NYC to consult. They've apparently made changes to the inventory. Not with just Ed Durango, but others. MR tasked Everett with sending me a list." Grimacing, he shoved his hands through his hair. "I'll have to personally call them all..."

Sage followed him back to the office, where the facts and figures awaited him. "I'm guessing these are all alterations in inventory that you don't agree with."

Nodding tersely, he slipped behind the desk and turned on the computer. "Then again, I don't know that much about what the socialites and inherited-money crowd buys."

"So you have to trust your partners," she guessed.

"I've put in too much time, effort and energy in this venture not to. But I hate letting the artisans and vendors I've personally contracted to do business with down."

Sage hated to see him betrayed, too. But there wasn't a whole lot she could do to help. Except be there for him.

"Nick went back to Dallas?" Lucille asked the following day, when she arrived to help Sage set up the nursery.

"Early this morning." Usually he left late Sunday evening, but this time he had delayed until the last possible moment and departed Monday morning. Part of it had been what she sensed was his reluctance to go back and deal with MR and the partners. The other half had been his continuing concern over her and the baby.

"How's Little One?" her mom asked sympathetically.

Sage sighed. "Still breech."

Lucille hugged her. "How's your back?"

With a shrug, Sage admitted, "Always kind of achy and uncomfortable, but the stretching and the prenatal yoga classes are helping." As was Nick's doting care. There was literally nothing as heavenly and soothing as one of his back massages. Except maybe a back massage followed by a hot lovemaking session...

Now, if only they could be together more than just the

weekend, life might really start to be as perfect as she wanted it to be...

"Ready to get started?" Lucille paused at the sight of the blanket and pillow Sage had forgotten to take off the sofa.

Sage lifted a hand, before her mother could read anything further into it. "I couldn't get comfortable last night, so Nick finally came out here to give me a little more room."

Her mother scanned Sage's queen-sized bed, where the covers were already neatly in place. Stacks of freshly laundered infant wear, blankets and crib sheets laid out.

"Nick's a big man."

No kidding. And handsome and sexy and kind and loving, to boot. "Six foot four." As well as way too big for her bed, even without her pregnant self in it. Casually, she told her mom, "I've been thinking about getting him a king-sized bed for Father's Day, for my apartment."

It would take up most of her bedroom, but they'd be able to sleep together just as comfortably here as they could at his ranch house. Always a plus. And still have their baby nearby.

"*Your* apartment," Lucille echoed, as if she had never heard the phrase.

Sage returned her mother's odd look. "Yes. The one we're standing in? You know, the one Dad gave me..."

Her mother did not look any happier.

Sage went still. "What about that bothers you?"

For a moment, she thought her mother wouldn't reply. Which again, was no surprise, since they had made a promise to each other, when the big scandal with the family foundation had hit the previous summer, to stop arguing so much about inconsequential things, and do their best to simply love and support each other.

Finally, Lucille said, "You want to give each other more furniture? For Mother's Day? *And* Father's Day?"

Why did everyone think it strange Nick had given her a set of ergonomic cooking stools for Mother's Day? she wondered. What should he have given her? A diamond engagement ring—albeit, a little belated?

"That was a sweet and thoughtful gift, Mom," she defended hotly. "Mine would show him that I care about his physical comfort, too."

Lucille shook her head as if that would clear it. "Physical comfort..." she repeated.

"Yes, Mom, what's wrong with that?" Sage winced at her snappish tone, aware her pregnancy hormones were getting out of whack again. Plus, the stress of the argument was causing her back to begin to ache!

Her mother's expression gentled. "I know Nick is concerned about you, sweetheart, and that you are equally concerned about him."

"Good." Because they were.

"What I'm curious about is, what kind of a Faustian bargain did you make?"

Sage flushed.

Her mother went on, "I never hear you say you love each other. For heaven's sake, you didn't even allude to it on your wedding day!"

So what? Sage tried not to huff. "Love isn't everything, Mom."

Lucille disagreed. "Then you married for what? Expedience? Propriety?"

Sage really didn't want to get into this, but since her mother had brought it up, she had no choice but to remind archly, "You were the one who didn't want me to have a baby on my own, if you remember."

Lucille laid a hand across her chest. "Because I wanted

you to *have it all*, Sage. The kind of romantic love and friendship that provides a foundation for a solid, enduring family."

The implied criticism stung.

Sage folded her arms in front of her and propped them on her rounded belly. "What makes you think Nick and I don't have that?"

Lucille picked up the diaper hanger and began filling it. "The fact that the two of you are still maintaining separate residences, with no apparent plans to merge into one. You still haven't told me—even now—that you love the man you've chosen to have a baby with."

Sage didn't know what to say to that.

Because although her feelings for Nick were deep and enduring, she also knew they had promised each other they wouldn't muddy the waters with impractical, elusive emotions and "fleeting" romance.

She and Nick had sworn they would stay in the best-friends zone. She couldn't—wouldn't—risk changing that at this late date. Not when they both had a baby they already adored on the way.

Sage picked up a stack of newborn undershirts and carried them to the changing table–dresser. "I don't know what to tell you, Mom," she said stiffly, opening the drawer. "Except that what Nick and I have together works. And will continue to work."

As long as they didn't change the rules at this late date.

THE FOLLOWING FRIDAY, Sage walked out of her prenatal yoga class to find MR standing in the hospital annex hallway. Surprised, she walked over to greet the statuesque Dallas executive. "Nick's not with me for this."

MR's glance raked the abundant maternal curves revealed by the clinging leotard and tights. "I know. He's over at Monroe's, with Everett and the PR people, getting photographed for the advertising backstory. I wanted a moment with you alone." MR held out a chai iced tea. "It's decaf."

Sage slung her rolled mat over one shoulder, then drew the thigh-length jersey cover-up closer to her body, momentarily forgetting the sultry heat she would face when she exited the building.

"Where would you like to go?" she asked with a resigned sigh.

"I have an air-conditioned car and driver, waiting."

Like that wouldn't draw a lot of attention.

Reminding herself this was for Nick, not the venture capitalist who had been making him miserable, Sage forced a smile. "Sounds good."

They walked in silence among the other pregnant women, until they got to the limo. MR gestured for Sage to go first.

Not sure she wanted to know what her rear view looked like, even with the cover-up, Sage climbed in.

The elegantly thin MR settled opposite her. "As Nick has probably told you, the grand opening of Upscale Outfitters will be on Saturday of Father's Day weekend. Many local dignitaries and celebrities, including the mayor of Dallas will be invited. The ribbon cutting will be at 9:45 that morning. We'd like your family to attend, Sage."

"Are you sure?" The store wasn't that big. "There are a lot of us. Nick has a brother and three sisters, plus in-laws and—"

"We're only talking the Lockharts, Sage."

Sage just looked at her, sure MR had to be kidding.

She was not.

MR removed her black eyeglasses. "The Lockharts

have ties to the Dallas community, and it's those very wealthy customers we are coveting."

"But it's Nick's venture. Surely his family should be there."

"The Monroe clan is 'small town.' They'd feel out of place. Plus, they'd add no value."

With effort, Sage managed not to tell MR what she thought of her. "Have you told Nick this?"

MR smiled tersely. "I was hoping, given your background, and position as his wife, that you could explain it to him."

"I don't agree with it. So, no. I'm not going to do that. It's either both full families are invited," Sage stated firmly. "Or no one is."

MR shrugged. "If you choose not to attend…"

Sage lifted a silencing palm. "I didn't say I wouldn't be there. I will," Sage told MR firmly. Nick was not just her best friend, he was her husband, and the father of her unborn child. She would support him all the way.

"So. When are you going to tell me what's going on with you?" Nick asked later that evening as the two of them walked the town green, ice-cream cones in hand.

Sage'd had a craving for hand-churned butter pecan. Nick had selected chocolate almond.

"You've practically had steam coming out of your ears all evening," he continued.

Sage hadn't realized he had noticed. But then, Nick always realized more than she would have preferred. It was what had initially drawn her to him, and what kept her from completely lowering her guard, too.

He pushed on. "Did MR say something to upset you?"

She always upsets me. But I'm not about to upset you,

too. "My lower back is bothering me," Sage fibbed. For once, it wasn't.

Nick squinted at her playfully, not fully buying it, but willing to play along—for the moment. "There's a cure for that, you know," he drawled.

Oh, she knew. Just thinking about making love with him again made her mouth water and her insides tingle.

"Ice cream first," she said. Then they could go back to her apartment, or maybe his ranch...

Catching her coveting his chocolate, Nick switched cones with her. For a moment, they savored the flavors in silence. "So what else?" he said eventually.

I'm tired, she was about to fib, when she felt something weird inside her. Very weird, as a matter of fact.

Nick squinted. "Sage?"

She sucked in a breath, took his free hand and put it on her waist, left of her navel. "Feel that," she whispered.

He went still. "Is that the baby?"

Sage nodded. "Kicking," she whispered, almost afraid to move for fear she would stop whatever was going on inside her.

"Or punching," she guessed with a grin. "And that can only mean one thing..."

Nick laughed, triumphant. "Little One is on the move!"

Chapter Twelve

"You're right," Dr. Johnson confirmed with a smile during Sage's checkup, Monday morning "Your baby is no longer in breech position."

"Which means all is well." It was all Sage could do not to break out into a happy dance. Beside her, Nick looked just as relieved.

Her obstetrician nodded. "Your weight is also on track, and the baby is growing at a healthy pace."

Nick, who was standing on the other side of the exam table, squeezed Sage's hand. Appreciating the way he supported her, Sage squeezed his hand back affectionately, then confirmed cautiously, "So a C-section won't be necessary."

The doc paused to make a note on her chart. "Never say never, but probably not, given the way things stand today."

Sage wasn't surprised to see that her overprotective husband still remained concerned. "Is there a possibility Little One could go back to a breech position, the same way he or she just turned around?" he asked.

Dr. Johnson paused. "It's possible, but unlikely. However, if you do feel the baby on the move again in the next day or so, Sage, let us know. Otherwise, the only thing this little tyke will do is grow bigger and heavier, and drop farther down into the birth canal to get ready for the big day." Which was now less than one month away.

Sage and Nick exchanged glances, giddy with excitement.

"I have another question," Sage said. And it was an important one. She told the doctor about Nick's grand opening in Dallas, Father's Day weekend. "I know it's a little less than two weeks away from the due date, but I'd like to go." She drew a bolstering breath. "Can I?"

MINUTES LATER, NICK and Sage exited the hospital annex. Looking prettier than ever in a summery pale peach dress that brought out the healthy hue of her cheeks, Sage stepped out into the bright sunlight.

Sage shot him a sidelong glance, as determined as he was wary. "I know you don't agree with my plan, but—" her lower lip slid out in the stubborn pout he knew so well "—you heard what Dr. Johnson said. It will be all right for me to go with you, *providing* I don't show any signs of early labor, and am checked by one of the obstetricians in his office the morning of departure, and get plenty of rest while I'm there."

She came closer, inundating him with a drift of perfume. "He's also going to give us the name of an obstetrics group and hospital close to the Galleria mall, and fax our records over in advance, so if anything does happen while we're in Dallas, we'll have someplace to go."

Nick knew all that, but it didn't stop him from worrying. "I don't want you to put yourself or the baby in jeopardy," he countered, all too aware how life could change in a heartbeat.

She winced as she stopped next to his pickup truck, and paused to rub the small of her back. "I'm not going to do that. I am, however, going to be at your side on what could be the biggest day of your life."

The three biggest days of his life had already happened. The first time they'd kissed and made love, thereby going from friends to lovers in one lightning moment, the day she had asked him to father their child and the day she had agreed to marry him.

Nick opened the door to let the heat out. Then reached over and massaged the tight muscles she'd been working on until she relaxed in blissful relief.

Sage smiled in the soft contented way she always did just after they'd made love.

His body reacted in kind. He wanted to make her his, then and there.

Sage smoothed a hand across his chest. She looked up at him cajolingly. "Besides, if I were going to go into early labor, wouldn't you rather I be with you, then two hours away by car?"

She had a point.

One he could not argue.

He had missed the ultrasound and he was sure as heck not missing the birth.

Just as important, this was what she wanted.

"Okay," he said gruffly, "you've convinced me."

She stood on tiptoe, wreathed her arms about his shoulders, and kissed him soundly. "Come back to my apartment," she whispered with a seductive smile, "and I'll let you convince me to do whatever pleases you, too."

She wasn't kidding, Nick found out a short time later.

They'd barely shut the door behind them, when she had toed off her flats, unzipped and shimmied out of her dress. Her pretty pink nipples tented the soft cotton fabric of her bra and her matching panties hit just below the enticing swell of her belly.

She came closer, already undoing the buttons on his shirt. "You can say no, you know."

He laughed at the notion as the blood pooled low. "Not much chance of that, sweetheart," he told her hoarsely, taking her hand and putting it over his fly.

Her golden-brown eyes shimmered in surprise.

Determined to show her just how important she had become to him, he pressed his lips to hers, until she curled against him in surrender, wanting more.

Heart pounding in his chest, he laid her down on the bed. While she watched, he stripped down to the buff, then divested her of every inch of clothing, too. Enjoying the soft, supple sight of her, he lounged next to her. She shivered in delight as he ran his hand over her body, from shoulder to breast to inner thigh, then arched as he found her most sensitive spot.

Closing her eyes, she let her head fall back. "I have to warn you," she purred as he stroked, and adored her with masterful precision, "it takes very little these days for me to go off like a rocket."

Her every quiver was like a match to flame. And though he sensed she was falling as hard and fast for him as he was for her, he also knew he had not yet enticed her to take their relationship to the next level.

He bent over to kiss her, savoring the soft, womanly taste of her. "Me, too. Which is why—" he kissed her again, even more passionately "—we have to…go slow…"

And go slow they did.

Taking it one step, one caress, one kiss at a time. Until there was no more waiting. Only wanting. Only the mewl of her mounting frustration and the need to be as close as they could possibly physically get, again.

Driven by the same relentless need, he moved behind her. Aware some positions had become uncomfortable for her, he rolled her onto her side, lifted her where she needed to be and slid between her thighs. Kissing the nape of her neck and caressing her languorously with his hand, he possessed her with easy, shallow strokes that were as tantalizing to her as they were for him.

Again and again, until the need to possess her heart and soul built to a fierce unquenchable ache. And still he loved her, slowly and deliberately, until she sighed and shuddered and called his name. And he lost control, too.

Replete with satisfaction, they stayed that way, wrapped up tight in each other's arms.

When the aftershocks stopped, he turned her to face him again. Their breaths catching, hearts beating in unison, she lifted her lips to his. Pleasure sifted through them anew. They kissed, softly and languidly, until both were ready to make love again.

And Nick knew, life just didn't get any better than this.

JUNE HIT TEXAS with a blast of heat that left the entire state reeling, and continued the entire first week. Air-conditioning helped, of course, but at eight months pregnant, Sage was still sweltering, even when the outdoor temperature hadn't topped 105 degrees every day.

Dallas was equally hot.

Concerned, Nick called every evening to make sure Sage and the baby were okay.

The calls were the highlight of his day.

Even when she only seemed to be half paying attention to him. "What are you doing?" he asked in exasperation, when another clattering noise interrupted their conversation.

"Um… Getting some ice from the icemaker."

She had just gotten ice two minutes ago, for her beloved decaf chai tea.

Before that, she had been standing in front of a fan, trying to cool off. And while he didn't fault her the extra cooling power of an oscillating stand fan, in addition to the central air-conditioning in her apartment, he was aggravated to only hear one out of every three words she was saying to him, due to the background noise.

"Can you repeat what you just said?" Nick asked. "I can barely hear you."

"I'm sorry." Sage sighed. The background noise faded slightly. The heat and complaint in her voice did not.

"I'm. Just. So. Hot. I really can't stand it."

He could imagine her beaded in sweat, the way she had been through most of the latter half of her pregnancy, especially when they were making love. Which they did every chance they got together.

Smiling affectionately, he attempted to tease her into a better mood. "Thought about taking a cold shower?"

"Already did. The minute I finished at The Cowgirl Chef. But, not to worry," she continued with a smugness that enticed, "my latest plan seems to be working."

The victory in her low voice had his senses humming. "And what might that be?" he returned.

"I'm running ice cubes down my body."

Just like that, he was hard as a rock and missing her so badly he could barely stand it. "Seriously?"

"Would I joke about this?" She sounded irritable again.

Wishing he could wrap his arms around her and pull her close, and kiss her until they both forgot why she was piqued, he settled on listening to the sound of her low, sexy voice.

"Why aren't we Skyping or FaceTiming right now?" he teased, already getting a pretty good visual in his mind.

"Because then you would see just how enormous I'm getting this week."

He shook his head, wishing she could see herself through his eyes. "You're beautiful," he said tenderly.

Unimpressed, she harrumphed. "I'm fat."

"Flat-out gorgeous."

"Portly."

"Stunning and amazing—"

She sighed loudly. "Let's go back to what we were talking about before we got sidetracked. What were you saying about your meeting first thing tomorrow?"

"It's a pitch for a group of potential investors for the second store." One they were still working on, as a matter of fact. He had just taken a break to call home.

"The one in Houston?" Sage prodded.

"Denver," he corrected.

An uncomfortable silence fell. Finally, Sage cleared her throat. "Did you say Denver—as in Colorado?"

He'd felt the same way when he heard the change in venue earlier that day.

For both their sakes he downplayed the inconvenience of the project location. "There's a new luxury mall going up there. It's slated to open in August. One of the original merchants, another upscale Western-wear store, had to drop out, so MR and the partners snapped up the space. Now we just have to find financiers to fund it."

Sage took a moment to process that. "Is it going to be just like the one in Dallas?"

He had shown her pictures of the interior in progress,

as well as let her peruse the upscale merchandise set to be in the store.

"MR and the partners have decided that each venue should have a different look entirely, suitable to the overall location. They want more of a boutique feel, instead of a chain." Which meant a whole truckload more work, from the outset. Most of which would likely have to be done on site.

"I see." Sage's tone was cool.

"I'm going to limit my travel there, Sage." That had already been decided.

More silence.

"Sage?" Was she angry? Had they been using FaceTime or Skype, he would have been able to see her expression and have a better idea of what she was thinking and feeling.

"I'm still here."

Yet, Nick noted, her voice sounded weak and thready. He began to panic, the way he always did when he was away from her and she might need him. "Are you okay?"

"Yes, ah…"

His heart stopped at the sound of her high-pitched yelp, followed by a low, tortured moan. "Sage?" Nick pressed again.

Another sound of distress. This one more intense.

"Tell me what's happening!" he demanded.

All he got was more silence.

"Right now, Sage," he warned, adrenaline racing, "or I'm calling 911…" Cell still pressed to his ear, he headed for the MEP office landline.

"No." Sage gasped again, and let out a frantic cry. "Don't do that!"

Nick stopped dead in his tracks. "*Are* you in labor,

Sage?" he could tell from the sound of things she was in pain.

He heard her draw a deep, halting breath.

"Yes. I think I am."

"YOU CAN'T LEAVE," MR said, when Nick went to the conference room where she and Everett were still working on the PowerPoint slides for the next day's presentations.

Did she have a hearing problem? Nick wondered, grinding his teeth in frustration.

"Sage is in labor."

The only reason he hadn't called 911 was because the contraction had passed, and her good friend, and sister-in-law Adelaide was on her way to take Sage to the hospital.

MR took off her glasses. "So? It's a first baby, Nick. Hence her labor and delivery can take anywhere from twenty-four to thirty-six hours on average."

There was nothing average about Sage. Or his baby, Nick thought fiercely.

"Which means—" MR consulted her watch "—since it's close to midnight now, you can still make our 10:00 a.m. meeting tomorrow, drive back to Laramie afterward and still get there in plenty of time."

Nick really did not have time for this. "I'm leaving."

Everett studied him, with his usual poker faced expression. He couldn't be sure, but Nick thought there was a small smile playing around the edges of the assistant's mouth. As if he were enjoying not seeing his boss get what she wanted, for a change.

MR leaped up, momentarily losing her cool. "Nick, if you bail on us again, there will be repercussions," she warned.

Nothing, Nick thought, like the ones that would happen if he missed the most important day in his life to date.

"Goodbye, MR."

He turned and walked out of the room, down the hall and out of the building.

He tried calling Sage again when he reached his car, but his call went straight to voice mail. "Sage, it's Nick, I love you and I'm on my way. I should be there in two and a half hours or less. Call me if you can."

Except, she didn't call.

And all the hospital would tell him was that she had made it to the ER, no problem, Adelaide by her side, and was being treated. And he should drive safely, as things still appeared to be in the *very early* stages. But, the nurse promised, she would call him if there were any changes.

So Nick drove, calmly and safely.

And thought about how much he wished he were already at his wife's side. Instead of miles away.

He reached the hospital at two thirty in the morning.

Walked in through the only doors open that time of night, the Emergency entrance.

And saw, to his surprise, Sage, standing in street clothes near the desk, her wheeled hospital bag on the floor beside her. She was completely red-faced and miserable. His older brother, Gavin, an ER physician, was standing with his arm around her shoulders. "…happens to a lot of people," he was saying.

Nick crossed the distance between them hurriedly. "What's going on?" he asked.

Sage could barely look him in the eye. "I wasn't in labor," she mumbled.

"She was having Braxton Hicks contractions," Gavin

explained. "We kept her under observation for a while, just to make sure."

"But it was all a false alarm. Apparently, I'm still a good three and a half weeks away from delivery," she said, then turned on her heel, still shaking her head in abject humiliation, and headed for the exit.

"Take her home," Gavin advised with a meaningful look. "See she gets *a lot of rest and TLC.*"

More than up for that, Nick grabbed the hospital bag Sage seemed to have forgotten and strode after her. He caught up with her as they reached the outside. The air was still stifling hot.

"I've never been so embarrassed in my life," she muttered as he opened her door for her.

"You'll feel better when we get to your apartment," he soothed.

Sage stopped, her mouth open in a round O of further distress.

Nick paused, not sure why she would find fault with that. "I figured you'd want to go there instead of the ranch since it's close, and bound to be way cooler, because I turn the AC way up when I'm away, but if you'd prefer to be at the ranch house…" With all the privacy…

"I'd rather be at my apartment. But…" She threw up her hands in frustration. "We probably shouldn't. Not without ruining everything else."

She was not making any sense. "What are you talking about?" Nick asked.

She shut her eyes, sighed and motioned him on. "You'll see."

WHEN THEY WALKED into her apartment and approached her bedroom, Nick could only stare.

"You don't like it," Sage guessed desultorily.

"What's not to like about a king-sized bed?" It was perfect for making love, cuddling. He wouldn't have to worry about taking up too much of the space, thereby exacerbating the back problems that had been plaguing her the entire pregnancy.

As if on cue, Sage put a hand behind her waist, rubbed. "It takes up most of the room."

He stepped behind her to take over the massage, gently kneading until he felt the knotted muscles on either side of her spine began to ease. "But what a way to take it up."

Sighing luxuriantly, she leaned into his touch.

Feeling her start to relax, he turned her to face him. "Why didn't you tell me you were doing this?"

"Because it was supposed to be a surprise for Father's Day, Nick." New misery lit her eyes. "Only I was going to have to give it to you *early*, since we're going to be in Dallas that weekend for the grand opening."

"I gave you the ergonomic kitchen stools a couple days early," he pointed out. Mostly because *he* hadn't been able to wait.

"I know. But when you saw your present for the first time, I wanted it to be completely made up with all the linens. Instead of just with the wrong-sized pillows, plain white sheets and a single blanket. But the accoutrements haven't come in yet, and won't get here until Thursday, so…darn it all—" she balled her fists at her sides "—why are you smiling?"

Joy rushing through him, he wrapped his arms around her. "Because this bed is the best present anyone has ever given me." It meant Sage wanted to get closer to him, the same way he wanted to get closer to her.

She blinked up at him, whispering, "Really?"

"Really," he confirmed thickly, hugging her close.

He cupped her chin and lifted her face to kiss her. Then stopped, when she burst into tears.

"You're sure we don't need to go back to the hospital," Nick asked, half an hour later, when Sage still hadn't stopped crying.

Her silent flow of seemingly unstoppable tears was really starting to worry him.

"It's j-j-just h-h-hormones," she cried, fisting her hands in his shirt. "And the fact that I'm just so tired of being pregnant, and hot all the time, and achy and moody. And the fact that I cry when I don't know why, and laugh when I shouldn't and never seem to get a full night's sleep." She hiccupped. "And I know I have a healthy baby and I shouldn't complain…"

Nick gathered her even closer, loving the feminine feel of her against him. "In your place, I'd complain, too."

"No you wouldn't," she argued, "because you're a saint."

He couldn't help it—he laughed at that. "Oh, Sage," he said, pressing a kiss in her hair as they snuggled together in their new king-sized bed. "If you only knew… how flawed I am."

"You aren't," she insisted stubbornly, beginning to sound a little sleepy now.

But he was.

Otherwise, he never would have pretended that they could be just friends, and then lovers, and then co-parents, and wife-and-husband-in-name-only and want nothing more from her than what she offered.

Because the truth was, he wanted a hell of a lot more from her. And from himself.

He wanted to be able to tell her how he felt without

fear of losing her. He wanted them to have it all. Marriage, a kid. Hell, half a dozen kids! And the kind of love that would last a lifetime, just like his parents had, and hers apparently had enjoyed, too.

But if that wasn't in the cards for them—and he had to admit, it increasingly looked like they would never move past the status quo—then he would have to find a way to be satisfied with what they had, and not waste time looking for anything more.

Because to do so could spoil everything. And that was the last thing he wanted.

Chapter Thirteen

"So what do you think?" Nick asked Sage, when he took her to the Galleria after hours for her first look at Upscale Outfitters.

"Very nice," she said.

And it was. The distressed white-and-beige brick walls contrasted nicely against polished floors with the patina of rich aged dark brown leather. The lighting was perfect, the strategically placed mirrors and carpeted dressing rooms of the finest quality. The expensive designer clothes, boots and hats were gorgeous, too.

Nick looked around. Pleased, and yet…

She came closer, inhaling his brisk masculine scent. "What is it?" she asked softly, taking his hand.

For a moment, they stood pensively side by side, linked by so much more than their entwined palms. Then he shook his head, as if kicking himself for looking a gift horse in the mouth. "Nothing."

When they had first become friends, they had told each other everything. Or so it seemed. Since they'd been married they had started censoring themselves from time to time. If it continued, she knew they would lose the intimacy that had bound them together thus far. And that scared her.

She drew a breath, then prodded, "Nick?"

For a moment, he remained silent. Seeming to do battle with himself, even as he studied his handiwork. Finally, he said in that sexy, gruff voice she loved, "There's nothing here of what I envisioned when I came up with the idea of turning Monroe's Western Wear into a chain of stores."

She swiveled to face him. "Maybe that's because the original Monroe's, with its century of service to one community, can't ever be duplicated," she soothed. "Even if the two stores were identical in every way."

His gaze drifted thoughtfully over the dark blue knit maternity shorts and top she wore before returning to her face. "You may have a point there."

Her body tingling with the need to make love with him, she sauntered even closer, glad they had the evening to themselves.

Curious, she had to ask, "Do you wish your family was going to be here tomorrow for the ribbon cutting?" The way hers had been when she'd opened The Cowgirl Chef. She searched his eyes. "Because it might not be too late to get them here, you know."

Nick vetoed the idea with a shake of his head. "MR was clear. No family."

Except mine, with their connections, Sage thought ruefully, glad Nick had never found out about that.

Nick walked over to straighten a display of top-of-the-line boots. "She doesn't want noncustomers taking up space that could be used for paying clientele. That's why only she and Everett will be here tomorrow, representing the other partners."

Doing her best to lighten the somber mood, Sage propped a hand on her hip, adapting a saucy stance. "Are you sure I'm invited then?" She batted her eyelashes flirtatiously. As he began to grin, she pushed on, "Or will it only be okay if I purchase something, too?"

He caught her around the waist and brought her as close as her pregnant shape would allow. He curved a hand over her cheek, then cupping her chin in his hand, he gently rubbed a thumb over her lower lip.

"You are nonnegotiable," he told her, his voice husky with affection. "And for the record, I'm very glad you're here to support me." He bent to kiss her lips. "I know it can't be easy for you, traveling in the last trimester."

Sage waved off the "sacrifice."

"It was no big deal," she insisted cheerfully. "I know I was a little weepy there for a few days earlier in the month," she admitted, playfully wrinkling her nose at him, "but I promise you, I've managed to put an end to the crying jags. In fact, I haven't had a single one since the night of the whole Braxton Hicks episode!"

Nick grinned as she laid her head on his shoulder, and he reached over to massage a hand down her spine. "You really have to stop feeling embarrassed about that."

Sage only wished she could.

Determined, however, to make sure it never happened again, that she would never jump the gun and mistake a few semiregular "practice" contractions for the real thing, she went back to talking about the trip.

"I know you've been a little nervous about me traveling with you, but there's really nothing to worry about." She reiterated what she had already told him, before they'd left Laramie County. "I saw the doctor this morning. He said Little One is still positioned fairly high up in my abdomen, and I'm not showing even a single sign of early labor. Which is what we'd expect, given that my due date is still another two weeks away."

"That's good," Nick interrupted, fiercely protective

as ever, "because if you were any closer to delivering our baby…"

He would have eighty-sixed her trip, for sure.

And it would have killed her not to be here with him, on his big weekend.

She brightened as they let themselves out the employees' entrance and walked out into the hallway that led to the exit.

"In any case," she reminded him, "the drive here was only a little over two and a half hours. And we stopped three times so I could get out and stretch and walk around. Plus—" she stopped to make a comical face "—followed every precaution ever known to pregnant women and their doctors."

He laughed at her dramatics.

Wrapping his arm around her shoulders, he tucked her into the solid heat of his body, then leaned down to press a kiss on the top of her head. "We still need to get you to the hotel so you can have a proper dinner and rest."

That sounded good.

Except…

Sage really hated to tempt fate.

She turned to face him as they stepped out into the heat of the Texas summer night. "Are you sure you want to return to The Mansion?" She drew an enervating breath. "I know the management promised us an amazing experience if we ever chose to return again, but… the last time didn't work out so well." She would hate for a repeat of their wedding night. And though she felt fine now, she was still prone to a little evening sickness, from time to time.

"I've taken pains to make sure everything will be perfect for you this time," Nick said. "Plus, it's near the hospital your obstetrician recommended—in case of any trouble, and right down the road from the Galleria mall, as well."

He'd made his case.

Sage smiled. "Then, The Mansion it is."

They were at the front desk, checking in, when the manager came out to speak to them.

Guessing—correctly as it happened—that she did not want to relive the specifics of her prior humiliation, Nick suggested gently, "Why don't you go on up to the suite with the bellman? I'll be along in a minute."

It had been a very long day for her and the baby, so she quickly relented. "I'll see you up there." She continued across the lobby with the bellman. Turned, as they reached the elevators.

Saw Nick's face.

Whatever was being said, he was definitely not happy.

She hoped that wasn't an omen of another bad night.

SAGE WAS STILL worrying when Nick walked into the hotel's best suite a good fifteen minutes later. "Everything okay down there?" she asked.

In the penthouse suite, it was just fine.

Both he and the hotel staff had gone all out to ensure that their stay was incredible. Bouquets of her favorite yellow roses adorned every room. There were baskets of fresh fruit and boxes of chocolate. An assortment of beverages. Sumptuous robes and slippers. As well as a complete array of spa services, should they request them.

He strolled toward her, confident as ever, a slow smile tilting the corners of his lips. "It's going to be perfect," he promised.

As if the grim exchange had never happened.

Sage studied him, not sure why he was suddenly shutting her out. Just knowing that he was. And it had something to do with his conversation with the hotel manager.

Unable to help but feel a little hurt, she slid him a look. "You sure?" She splayed her hands across his chest. Aware she didn't want him lying to her, for any reason, she savored the strong, steady beat of his heart. "'Cause you didn't look very pleased earlier."

For a second, his face bore the look of a warrior about to head into battle. Then, he became inscrutable again. Wrapping his arms about her, drawing her in close against him, murmuring huskily, "I was just making sure there would be no shrimp or fish of any kind in the room service dinner they are sending up for us."

Her inner radar told her that while that might be true, it was also a little more than that. But then, given what had happened during the previous visit, she figured he had a right to be overly cautious. Especially since the health of their baby was also at stake.

Not about to let the past calamity keep them from having a great time tonight, however, she snuggled against him. "I'm sure it will all be fine. But if it makes you feel better," she teased, "I'll let you check everything out in advance, just to be sure."

He tilted her face up to his. Their lips met and they kissed, soft and deep and slow, getting their evening alone off to an excellent start.

An hour and a half later, after what had turned out to be the most wonderful dinner she'd ever had was winding down, and they walked out to the penthouse terrace overlooking the city, Sage could still feel an undercurrent of something going on with Nick.

"Can I ask you something?"

He lounged against the brick wall, the starlit sky and sea of glittering city lights forming a romantic backdrop behind him. Crossing his arms, he flashed her a wolfish grin. "Anything."

Sage stationed herself opposite him, as the warm, dry summer air blew across their bodies. "Why were you so insistent we stay at a five-star hotel this evening?" she asked curiously. When it was so unlike anything he usually did for himself. "Was it because it's a big weekend for you? Or was it because you were trying to please me? And you somehow got the idea that this was what I required in terms of luxury and comfort?"

He sobered, confirming her worst suspicions. "You grew up with a lot of money, Sage."

Too much, she often thought in retrospect. "So therefore I'm above staying at the kind of modestly priced chain hotel, where you usually stay, when you're on your own?"

He paused, as ruggedly sexy as always. Looking deep into her eyes, he took her hand. "I want you to be happy."

Reveling in the strong warmth of his fingers encircling hers, she reiterated, "Money isn't going to make me feel that way, Nick. My parents realized that, too, which is why they put most of their accumulated wealth into the family's charitable foundation before my father died, and gifted my mother and me and my siblings all with property in Laramie County instead. So we would have a foundation to build our futures on. A future that would require each and every one of us to work and work hard for whatever we have. Just like my parents had to do."

He continued to hold her gaze, the corners of his mouth barely turning up. "We talked about that when we first became friends," he reminded, a veil dropping over his emotions.

Determined to understand him, the way a wife should, she leaned in even closer. "Then why do you think I still need to go back to the old life I had in Dallas growing up, the life where whatever I wanted, whenever I wanted it, was pretty much just given to me, no questions asked?"

He lifted his broad shoulders in a careless shrug, challenging her now. "Because that kind of life is hard to leave behind."

"Who told you that?" she countered irritably, then blurted out before she could stop herself, "MR?"

His manner as composed as hers was irritable, Nick inclined his head. "We had a few talks about downward mobility in general, early on. But to be honest," he said gruffly, "I was thinking about it long before that. Worrying that I might not be able to…" He stopped abruptly, started again, "That *you* might not be content with less, long-term."

Sage thought about the relief she'd felt, when she had left her moneyed childhood existence and struck out on her own after culinary school. Her needing to not be caught up in all that was part of what'd had her chasing her ex all over the West Coast, searching for a simpler version of happiness.

Was the opposite driving Nick now?

Was that part of the reason he'd let those with more wealth and power obliterate his vision for a chain of Western-wear stores, and replace it with their own?

Though he had every reason to be proud of what he had accomplished in getting the Upscale Outfitters chain started, she sensed he still felt frustrated and hemmed in. Maybe even more so than before he had signed a contract with Metro Equity Partners.

Because then he'd still had his dreams.

He hadn't had to cede creative and business control of the venture for greater financial stability in the long run. Just to protect his unborn child. And possibly please her, too…?

He tucked a strand of hair behind her ear. "I want you to have everything your heart desires."

Then that would be you, Nick, she thought wistfully, gazing into his eyes.

As more than friend or lover or husband-for-business-purposes-only. "I want you to have everything you ever wanted, too." She pushed the words through the ache in her throat. "And for the record, I am very happy in Laramie."

She yearned to add, *You could be, too, if you'd just stop chasing the almighty dollar and give it a chance.*

But wanting to support him in whatever he endeavored, she said kindly instead, "But I understand why you'd want something different from what you had growing up, too. Maybe," she added, attempting to look at it from his point of view, "in a way, we all do."

AND YET, NICK THOUGHT, as Sage slipped into the bathroom to get ready for bed, there were also plenty of things they both wanted. Friendship. An ongoing sexual relationship. This baby. And the sense of family Little One was already providing.

Initially, that had been more than enough to make him happier and more content than he had ever been.

That had begun to change the night they said their vows.

Although they had yet to share space together full-time, occasionally living together as husband and wife added another layer of intimacy to their complex arrangement. Sharing the ups and downs of her pregnancy, attending her obstetrical appointments and anticipating the birth of their child brought them closer, too. She wasn't just the wife in their for-business-reasons-only marriage, she was the wife he had always yearned to have. Sweet, loving, generous.

Definitely worth waiting for, he thought, as the bathroom door opened, and Sage walked out.

She was wearing one of the old-fashioned knee-length nightshirts he adored, with a band collar and a row of buttons up the front. Her face scrubbed of makeup, her cheeks a pretty pink, her just-brushed hair loose and flowing, she looked sweet and innocent, and, as she had been of late, incredibly shy about her body.

Although not about to admit it.

"I know." She rested one hand on her hip, and adapted a pinup girl pose. She fluffed the ends of her hair with her free hand. "I've still got it."

Grinning, he crossed to her side, and took her in his arms. "You better believe you do, sweetheart." He caressed the curve of her cheek with the pad of his thumb, as her lower lip trembled once again.

Then he lowered his mouth to hers, and kissed her long and slow and deep, before dancing her toward the bed. They broke apart long enough for him to gently lay her down.

He opened the buttons on her nightshirt, raining kisses over her face, her throat, her full, sexy breasts. She shivered as he went lower still. As his hands stroked and caressed, he kissed her in a way that let her know there would be no more holding back, no more pretending they weren't as important to each other as life itself.

Valiantly, Sage tried to keep her emotions out of the kiss. With absolutely no success. It didn't matter what deal they had made, long ago. Or how she longed to give him every ounce of freedom and independence he deserved.

When she was in Nick's arms, all she could think about, all she could do, was surrender. To the sensations his lips and hands created. To the hardness of his body, and the tender resolve in the way he made love to her.

She wanted to feel connected to him, not just physically, but heart and soul.

And when sensations ran riot through her, perspiration beading her body, and they finally reached completion and catapulted into oblivion, she had never felt more blissful.

Eventually, Sage's racing heartbeat slowed, and her body stopped shuddering. Sweet moments passed as they clung together. She sighed with contentment. If this wasn't true love, and she guessed it still wasn't, at least not in the traditional sense, she did not care.

Her relationship with Nick was everything she had ever wanted and needed. And in the end, wasn't that all that really mattered?

Nick smoothed a hand through her hair, down her spine.

He pressed a kiss into her hair. "Think you'll be able to sleep tonight?" he murmured, helping her put her sleep shirt back on and adjust the pillows, just so.

"I hope so," Sage said, yawning, as Nick shrugged on a pair of pajama bottoms and climbed in beside her.

She really needed it.

Chapter Fourteen

The only problem was, Sage didn't sleep. Despite the effort Nick had made to help her relax and get comfortable, she never really did get cozy in the big, wonderful hotel bed. Long after he was sound asleep, she was still staring at the ceiling. By morning, she was not just tired, she was unbearably cranky and out of sorts, too. To the point where every single pep talk she tried to give herself failed miserably.

And though she tried to hide it from Nick, she knew he had seen her unusually intense irascibility, too.

Finally, he asked what they were both thinking.

"Are you sure you want to go this morning?" He stood in the bathroom doorway. "Because I would understand if you didn't want to endure what could very well be a madhouse, if anywhere near the expected customer traffic comes thru."

This is his day. It has to go well. More important still, I want to be there for him.

"Yes, of course, I want to go." Sage slipped on a sleeveless, knee-length black jersey maternity dress that was supposed to be slimming but in reality clung to her enormous stomach, making her look and feel like a beached whale. "I am going to go," she repeated emphatically.

Nick studied her reflection. Zeroing in on her frown, he asked, nonplussed, "What's wrong?"

Nothing and everything, Sage thought, blinking back a new round of unprecedented tears.

She did not know why she was so crazy hormonal this morning. It was one thing to do without a little much-needed sleep. Another to cry in the shower, cry while trying to put on her makeup—to the point where she had to wash her face and do it all over again. All for no reason she could fathom!

Didn't she have the most wonderful man on earth by her side, waiting excitedly to welcome their baby into the world?

Hadn't he pampered her silly last night?

Made love to her with exquisite tenderness?

Helped her feel every bit as important to him as he was to her?

So why, then, Sage thought on a new burst of frustration, as she ran a brush through her freshly blown-dry hair, did she feel on the verge of losing it all over again?

Ducking his searching gaze, she padded back into the dressing area of the luxury suite, in search of the flats that went with the dress. She plucked them from the suitcase, and dropped them onto the floor. "I'm just excited for you," she fibbed.

Nick watched as she toed them into position, then attempted unsuccessfully to slip her swollen feet into them.

Nick knelt before her, like a prince courting his Cinderella. "Need some help, sweetheart?"

Unfortunately, he could not fit her feet into the soft ballet flats, either.

Not sure what she was supposed to do, with them just minutes away from departure, she contemplated her options. The sneakers she'd traveled in were too beat up. The only other thing she had were flip-flops.

Nick followed her gaze. "They'll be okay." He helped her slip her feet into them.

Aware it was supposed to be a brutally hot June day, with the temperature soaring to 104 degrees, but the mall itself might feel cool, she grabbed a lightweight sky blue cardigan and her bag.

Together, they headed out.

"I'm supposed to be there from open to close today, but MR is going to have a driver ready to take you back here, whenever you're ready," Nick said.

"Sounds good," she replied.

What wasn't good was the look on MR's face when she saw Sage walk into the luxury store, in flip-flops. As usual, the venture capitalist recovered quickly. Her disdain slipped into a warm, welcoming smile as she motioned for one of the sophisticated saleswomen. "You know what would go great with that dress? A summery white denim jacket and some black-and-peacock-blue boots."

"Absolutely," the clerk said. "I'll get right on it."

Her lower back aching, the way it had for months now, Sage let herself be led off. Behind her, she heard Nick tell MR, "I've got a few things I'd like to discuss."

"We'll talk in the back office," MR chirped happily.

The two disappeared, and Sage focused on being the "wife" Nick needed her to be.

NICK HELD HIS temper while MR shut the door behind them. Turning, she gave him a droll look. "Why so serious?"

Nick folded his arms in front of him. Curious as to

how long she'd play innocent. "I spoke to the manager at The Mansion last night."

MR's expression remained guileless. "And...?"

He'd known for months that his business partner was not the person she purported to be. But for her to stoop as low as she had was still unfathomable. At least for someone like him who had grown up in a rural community where neighbor looked out for neighbor.

"Cut the bull, MR," he retorted, his patience exhausted. "I know what you did."

MR walked over to the mirror she'd installed and checked out the black lace-over-silk dress and knee-high lace-up boots she wore. Adjusting the turquoise-and-leather pendant she wore, she turned back to face him, her countenance calm. "I'm sure I don't know what you're talking about."

Nick was just as sure she did. "Here's the bottom line. I'm done being jerked around like a marionette on a string."

MR paused, an exaggerated expression of sympathy on her perfectly made-up face. Carefully, she began, "I understand you're anxious about today."

Anxious, hell! "My wife and child are not going to be collateral damage in your ambitious schemes."

An unpleasant pause, filled with unexpressed guilt.

MR lifted a discerning brow, her countenance turning ugly. "Careful, Nick, this is a situation that could play out in more than one way." She arrowed a thumb at her sternum. "I'm the one with all the advantages."

Before he could continue, the sales rep knocked and opened the door slightly. At MR's approving nod, she walked in, a flushed Sage at her side. With a sweeping gesture toward Nick's wife, the clerk asked, "What do you think? Hat or no hat?"

MR's gaze narrowed critically, all business once again. "None for Sage. The custom, definitely, for Nick."

He couldn't help but note how beautiful and alluring Sage looked in the fancy boots and jacket. He also noted she had her right hand behind her, discretely rubbing the small of her back. A small bead of perspiration dotted her brow. He crossed to her side in instant concern, and wrapped a supportive arm around her waist. "Are you too hot in that?"

"I'm fine." She flashed a dazzling smile, her brow growing ever damper, as she rested against him. "I wouldn't mind sitting down for a moment, though."

Everett appeared in the doorway. "Several hundred people are already lined up outside the door and the camera crew is here to film the ribbon-cutting ceremony for the grand opening. The mayor just arrived, too."

MR handed Nick the hat they all wanted him to wear. "Nick?" Her shrill voice rang with impatience.

"Sage and I will be right there," he promised, already getting his wife a bottle of sparkling water from the fridge.

MR flashed her disapproval. "Five minutes," she warned.

"No problem."

Once he and Sage were alone, Nick took another long look at her. She seemed a little unsteady. And very tired, beneath the aura of flushed excitement. Protectiveness rose within him. "Are you sure you're up to this?" he asked her gently.

"Positive." She hesitated, her lip taking on a perplexed curve. "When I walked in, were you and MR arguing about something?" When he didn't answer right away, she added anxiously, "It sounded...unpleasant."

It likely would have been, had he gotten to the bottom line. But he figured that could wait. What was important now was Sage and their baby, making sure they both were okay.

"Nothing you need to worry about," he soothed. He would take care of this.

For all of them.

SAGE WASN'T SURPRISED Nick brushed her off. He had a way of shutting down emotionally whenever their inter-actions headed into overly intimate territory.

Still, it stung.

Luckily, they had no chance to pursue the conversa-tion, given Everett's repeat appearance in the doorway.

"Showtime!" the assistant said.

Gallantly, Nick offered Sage a hand up.

Obediently, Everett reminded him, "The hat."

With a grimace, Nick settled it on his head.

One hand on Sage's back, he escorted her out to the front. On the other side of the glass, a big white ribbon had been stretched across the space.

He dropped his hold on her as the mayor and other local dignitaries greeted him and offered their congrat-ulations. The camera crew filmed while Nick and MR jointly held the large pair of scissors and cut the ribbon. Everyone clapped. There were several hoots and hollers and loud whistles. The doors were pushed all the way open and the crowd, buzzing with excitement, surged inside.

It was, Sage noted, both gratifying to see such enthusiasm—even if the mercantile wasn't what Nick had originally envisioned—and a little overwhelming, too. Plus, maybe it was the unusually high heels of the boots she wore, but her lower back was now aching like the jab of a hot poker.

Warning herself that this event wouldn't last all that

long, she forced herself to smile through the near rhythmic discomfort.

Nick appeared at her side. "Mayor, I'd like you to meet my wife, Sage Lockhart Monroe."

The handsome politician nodded, extending his hand. "I know your family well."

"Very nice to see you here," Sage returned politely.

Then froze, as a river of something wet and warm trickled down her leg and splattered on the floor.

She looked down in horror and shock, as everyone around her automatically stepped back.

For a moment, she thought she had done the unthinkable and wet herself.

Then she knew.

Oh, heavens.

Oh, no.

Not now.

Not here.

My God…

"Sage?" Nick said, as the water saturated her underwear and dripped down her thighs.

She panicked as she felt her knees buckle beneath her.

A collective gasp filled the air. Nick rushed in and caught her as she fell backward. "It's okay. I got you… Talk to me, Sage. Can you tell me what's happening?"

"I need…to lie down…" she whimpered, and he eased her gently onto the floor. As pain wrapped her middle in a breath-robbing vice, she felt another even more disturbing sensation. She gripped her husband's forearm tightly. That couldn't be…could it? Oh, no. "Nick…" *My God!* "Nick…!"

He grabbed a folded sweater from a nearby display and eased it under her head. "It's all right, sweetheart, I promise. I'm right here with you, and I'm not going any-where. Someone's already calling 911…"

Too late for that, she thought miserably, as the panic and fear inside her twisted and rose. Tears blurred her eyes. "I feel the baby's head."

OUT OF THE corner of his eyes, Nick saw MR and Everett and their bevy of salesclerks taking charge and waving the crowds back.

Unfortunately, all the commotion caused even more people to gather outside the storefront.

For once glad the venture capitalist had such a take-charge personality, Nick turned back to his wife.

Drawing on everything he had learned about child-birth, he soothed, "You can't, sweetheart. It's way too soon for that."

Her eyes were glazed with panic and pain. "I do, I swear! It…" She moaned, a deep, feral cry for help, and gripped his arms, hard. "The baby is coming!"

Now? Here?

Sage held on even tighter. Wildly, she pleaded with him, "You've got to help me make sure…" She let out another panicked, keening cry. "You've got to look…"

Nick was vaguely aware they were moving racks of shirts around them, to try to block the view.

He got down on his knees, eased Sage's hem up, reached beneath her dress and removed her drenched panties. Easing her thighs apart, he inhaled a bolstering breath and checked.

Sure enough, she was right, it was definitely their baby's head.

Little One was crowning.

There was no time to wait for the EMTs.

"Get me something to put underneath her," he shouted, as Sage sobbed and panted.

Several brand-new extra-large men's shirts of fine soft cotton were ripped off hangers and thrust at him.

"Nick," Sage sobbed. "I've…got…to…push…"

He had no choice but to cede all control. "Then go for it, sweetheart," he said, hastily making a bed beneath her.

She grunted, shoved.

The head came out, into his waiting palm.

"Again," he directed, gently but firmly supporting the emerging infant.

She pushed.

The rest of their baby's body slid out into his waiting hands. Perfect as could be, and covered in a waxy white substance. The cord was still connected to Sage.

Sage lifted her head and shoulders off the floor, trying to see. "Nick…?" she asked anxiously.

"It's a boy," he declared.

And Little One hadn't made a sound, Nick noted in alarm. Didn't seem to be breathing, at all.

Sending up a silent prayer, Nick used the tip of his little finger to wipe the baby's nose and mouth of mucous, then held their infant upright.

Startled into awareness, their son let out a lusty, high-pitched cry.

Sage began to sob, openly now, and Nick felt a surge of love and gratitude as the paramedics rushed in.

The hours that followed were a blur. Sage had only hazy memories of the ambulance ride to the hospital and their time in the ER before being whisked up to the maternity wing.

But she would never forget the moment when she had seen Nick help their son take his first breath. Or the way he had looked as he settled their child in her arms. As if all his dreams had come true, too. Or the incredible miracle of cradling her baby son in her arms for the very first time. And the feeling of the contentment that flowed through her when the three of them were finally settled in one of the hospital's private maternity suites was beyond compare.

Nick sat in the chair next to the bed as she nursed. He watched, mesmerized, as little Shane fed.

Sage could tell he had something on his mind.

She did, too, so she decided to go first before any more time elapsed. "I'm sorry I disrupted the grand opening."

He shook off her apology. "I'm sorry I let them set the grand opening so close to your due date."

Sage shrugged. "With a 49 percent share, you didn't really have a lot of choice. And Father's Day weekend was a great time to enter the retail market." She expected the weekend sales would be through the roof. Not a bad way to start a business.

Nick, however, did not appear to be thinking about his hard-won success.

Brow furrowing, he let his gaze drift lazily over her. "Did you suspect you might be in labor this morning? Is that why you were so weepy?"

So he had seen her surreptitious tears, she thought, her body warming everywhere his gaze had landed. "My hormones were definitely raging," she admitted self-consciously, appreciating his tender concern, "but I wasn't having contractions. Not like I did when we had the whole Braxton Hicks debacle. Just the kind of lower back pain I've had the entire pregnancy. And I didn't connect that with labor." She grimaced, remembering. "Until my water broke, anyway."

Nick exhaled, his relief as strong as her own. "Thank heaven EMS got there quickly."

She grinned. "Thank heaven *you* knew exactly how to proceed until they *did* arrive."

He chuckled fondly, his attention moving from her to their son, and back again. "It's not like I had to do much," he admitted with an ornery grin. "When our son was ready to make his entry into the world, he came right on out."

They smiled and held hands. Then Sage handed their son over to Nick, to hold and burp. He had never looked so strong or handsome, or felt so very much an integral, needed part of her life. And Shane's... "We are so very lucky," she told him softly, meaning it with all her heart and soul.

One big hand gently cupping Shane's head and neck, the other supporting his diapered bottom, Nick tenderly cradled Shane against his broad chest. "We are," he admitted happily.

He kissed them both, then drew back, sober now, and looked her in the eye. "Which is why I want to make some changes in my business dealings. And most important, stop all the traveling right now."

Heaven knew, there was nothing Sage would like better than to have her husband around full-time, instead of just on weekends. But...

"Will the partners allow that?" she asked.

Nick's jaw jutted out. "It's not really their decision to make," he said curtly.

Wasn't it?

Sage wondered.

Chapter Fifteen

"Is now a good time?" MR asked, from the doorway of the hospital room, five hours later.

For celebrating it sure was, Sage thought, cuddling her newborn son in her arms. She just wasn't sure she wanted to do so with MR, who continued to annoy her on nearly every level. But with Nick's business partner standing there with a huge basket of baby things in her arms, and a congratulatory smile on her face, there wasn't much she could do but say, "Yes. Of course." With her free hand, Sage motioned her in.

"I won't stay long." MR set the luxurious gift on a chair and perched on the window ledge.

The exec had changed out of the Western wear she'd worn earlier in the day, and was now in the usual sleek business suit and heels. Her hair and makeup looked freshly done, too. In contrast to Sage, who still felt like a sweaty, disheveled mess, after giving birth.

MR continued scanning the room thoughtfully. "Where's Nick?"

"He went back to the hotel to get cleaned up and retrieve our hospital bag." So she could shower and change into something more comfortable than her hospital gown. Maybe do her hair and makeup, too.

She knew it was silly, but she wanted to look good for Nick—and Shane.

MR beamed. "Good. Then you and I will have a moment alone."

Feminine instinct told her this could not be good. Wary of the sweetly sleeping babe in her arms, Sage tried not to tense. "Something wrong?"

"Actually, for once in this process, everything is incredibly right! Shane's dramatic entry into the world has caused a *huge* media splash. We've been fielding calls right and left with news crews wanting to do stories on his birth. The sooner, the better, if we want to take advantage of this publicity gold mine. But Nick, as usual, is refusing to cooperate."

Good for my husband, Sage thought fiercely.

Family first. Always.

Deciding it best to be honest, she admitted calmly, "I don't think it's a good idea, either." Sage shifted little Shane higher in her arms. His little rosebud lips worked soundlessly for several seconds, before he let out a soft sigh, stuck his thumb in his mouth, just the way he had in her womb, and promptly fell back asleep. "Shane went through an incredible trauma, being born in the middle of a mall store."

"A luxury Western-wear emporium," MR corrected. She gave the infant a dismissive glance. "And he's fine!"

Technically, yes. But that didn't mean Sage wanted to trot her newborn son out like a pony on parade in front of a bunch of strangers. For mercenary reasons, no less!

But knowing MR would not understand that, she simply said, "I'm exhausted, too."

MR went over and shut the door to the hall. Their privacy ensured, she strode back to the foot of Sage's hospital bed. "I don't think you understand what an incredible opportunity this is to promote not just the opening of the first Upscale Outfitters store, but Nick as modern-day Western hero and all-around Renaissance man. Ruggedly handsome, sexy. Rancher-businessman. Loving husband and protective dad, who also turned out to be very good in a medical emergency."

That he had been, Sage thought proudly.

In fact he was so good, she was beginning to think she just might have finally disregarded all her heartfelt internal warnings and fallen head over heels in love with him, anyway.

Meanwhile, MR waxed on enthusiastically, "I mean, there he was, catching his son in his bare hands—on Father's Day weekend, no less!—and then wrapping him in one of our shirts, which, by the way, we have already sold out of. The partners will be *very* upset if Nick does not take advantage of this phenomenal stroke of good luck and publicize the heck out of what happened this morning."

Sage imagined that was the case. Her father had felt the same way about making money. Only to figure out in the end that in doing so he'd missed out on an awful lot along the way, particularly with his family.

"The news stations are promising to run Nick's interview and story all day tomorrow, in honor of the holiday." MR rubbed her hands. "All we have to do is get Nick to cooperate, pronto." She leveled a hard, expectant look at Sage.

She thought about the way MR had treated Nick the last few months, with her endless demands and constantly disregarding his decisions. Sage decided that deal or no, she did not owe MR anything. At least not of this import.

"I'm sorry, MR, but if Nick has already said no..."

MR's expression turned unpleasant. "Then overrule

him! As his 'wife' you certainly have that prerogative. There are two breaking news crews downstairs, waiting for my call. I can have them up here in five minutes to do a quick story with you and the baby, and then we can add Nick in, when he gets here. By then, it will be a done deal, so there will be no reason for him not to cooperate."

Sage had dealt with reporters during her family's scandal the previous summer. It was never that short, or easy, or uncomplicated. "I can't and won't override Nick on this," she reiterated firmly.

MR looked furious. "You understand this will be a deal breaker for the partners."

Sage doubted that.

If there was big money at stake, and if Nick was essential to make that cash, the partners would remain all-in.

Able to bluff as well as MR, she shrugged. "I can't help the way you and your partners feel."

MR tapped her foot impatiently. "No, but you can keep Nick from making a rash decision that will ruin his life."

Tired of the veiled and not-so-veiled threats, Sage looked the venture capitalist in the eye. "What are you trying to say?"

"If Nick wants his business dreams to come true, he's going to have to live up to his end of the deal he made. And be the face and driving force behind Upscale Outfitters."

"You can't be serious."

"Oh, but I am." MR went on, sweet as pie, "Because I'll tell you right now, the partners will either pull the funds on the rest of the projected stores, or force him to resign and give up his interest in the company. And that's if they don't sue him for breach of contract. And while Nick might think doing this his way, in his own time, is what he really wants right now, eventually he will realize what he gave up, Sage. He'll recognize that this was a once-in-a-lifetime opportunity. And he blew it out of some misguided notion of being there for you and your son.

"And when that happens," MR continued vindictively, "he'll go back to feeling as trapped as he was the day I met him. And it won't be me he resents, Sage. It'll be you and your son."

Sage stared at the executive. Wishing she could refute everything MR was saying, yet knowing in her heart it was true. Nick was just like her late father. Made for bigger things. No matter how much he loved his family and wanted to be with them, he would never be happy running one small store, in a small town. No matter what he said now.

And a Nick who was miserable would not be a good father, good friend or lover. Never mind husband...even if in name only.

Sage sighed in defeat. "What do you want me to do?"

"Make him do what he has to do. For all your sakes." MR paused. Looked down at Shane, then back at Sage. "You owe Nick this."

Much as Sage wanted to disagree, she could not.

SAGE'S HOSPITAL BAG in one hand, a bouquet of flowers and a teddy bear in his other, Nick burst out of the hospital elevator. Frowning, he stopped at what he saw. One camera crew going into the hospital room where Sage and Shane were supposed to be resting, another coming out.

MR walked out, and waved him toward them. "Here comes our hero now!" she gushed.

Nick strode forward, the fury and resentment inside him building. The knowledge he'd made a mistake, ever getting involved with MR and Metro Equity Partners, was stronger than ever.

A microphone was pushed into his face. "Nick! How does it feel to have delivered your own son on such an exciting day, no less!"

He might not want to be doing this. On the other hand, if he snarled, that would make headline news, too. He did not want that to be the lasting legacy of this amazing moment in his life.

Nick summoned the feeling of catching his son in his hands. Seeing little Shane take his first breath, and let out that strong, indignant cry. "It felt great!" Nick smiled, pushing on into the room.

Sage was propped up in her hospital bed, their infant son cradled lovingly in her arms. He wasn't sure which one looked more sweet and vulnerable, he just knew they were the center of everything good and solid and wonderful in his life.

He crossed to her bed, bent down and kissed her temple. Not for the cameras, but because he sensed she needed his support right now more than ever.

For a second, she relaxed into his touch. Her yearning to be alone, just the three of them, seeming as strong as his.

As he drew back, he saw her lower lip quiver.

"I think Little One is starting to get hungry again," she warned.

Which probably meant, Nick thought, there'd probably be a little crying again, and a huge need for privacy.

The news reporter motioned her camera crew closer. "Then we'll make it quick," she promised with a smile.

With MR looking on triumphantly, they went over the events of the morning. "And your baby's name is…?"

"Shane Lockhart Monroe," Sage and Nick said proudly together.

"Lovely! That's a wrap. Thanks so much, guys."

The crew exited. The other TV crew came back in briefly, asked a couple of questions specifically of Nick, got a thirty second film clip of the new family, and then departed.

No sooner had they cleared the portal than MR pulled out her smartphone. "Nick, we need to go over the calendar of events in Denver later this week."

Nick saw his wife deflate. "Not now," he said, as his son wrinkled his nose and began to shift and fuss.

MR stepped closer and folded her arms pertly in front of her. "I understand you'll have to take the baby back to Laramie when he's released tomorrow or the following day," she said kindly, "but after that, we're still going to need you in Colorado."

MR was right. They did have a lot to talk about. But he needed to speak to Sage first.

"I'll call you as soon as I can," he told the venture capitalist.

"Tonight?" MR pressed.

Nick wanted this done, too.

More than he ever could have imagined.

"I'll let you know where and when," he said.

HER EMOTIONS IN TURMOIL, Sage waited until Nick had closed the door, then draped a blanket over her shoulder and eased the gown down to expose one breast.

She cupped Shane's downy-soft head in her palm, and teased his lips with her nipple, until he latched on. Seemingly as adept at everything he tried as his father, he fed like a champ.

"You don't have to stay, you know," she said.

Especially when you're looking at me—and Shane—like that. As if we're everything you ever wanted or dreamed of having. Because it's moments like these, when I'm tempted to believe that the baby and I could be enough to make you completely happy, that also make me want to go off the rails and tell you how much I feel. In my heart and soul. And how much more I want in this life we're building together.

But she couldn't do that, Sage reminded herself sternly. Not without breaking the promises they had made to each other at the outset.

She knew Nick deserved better than that.

He flashed her a sexy, sidelong grin. "If you're shy, I don't have to watch," he volunteered kindly, moving a slight distance away. "I can sit over here. Or even head out to get you a decaf chai iced tea, if you like."

Sage blushed and shook her head as the unprecedented awkwardness between them increased. "It's not that." He was as familiar with her body as she was with his.

He turned to squint at her expectantly. "Then…?"

Ignoring the ache in her heart, Sage forced herself to do the right thing. With effort, she met and held his gaze. Reminding herself they were on the brink of having something truly wonderful, but only if they didn't get in the way of each other's dreams.

She swallowed, reining in the tremor in her voice, and looked him right in the eye. "You have business. This is still opening weekend and the new store will be open for several more hours." He had been slated to be there all day, as well as from 1:00 p.m. to 6:00 p.m. on Father's Day.

Nick pulled up a visitor chair, turned it around backward and sat down, legs straddling the seat, arms folded along the top. She noted he had put on the usual

American-made shirt and jeans, instead of the Italian-made brand he'd been wearing for the grand opening.

He smiled tenderly, watching as she moved Shane to her other breast.

"That's what I want to talk to you about," he said quietly, as she began to nurse their son again. His expression sober, he continued, "I've been mulling my options for a while now, but when you went into labor this morning, and I realized that the only reason you weren't at the hospital in Laramie, where you should and would have been, was all my doing, I also realized a lot had to change." He paused and compressed his lips together tightly. "I can't put family second, Sage. Not anymore."

NICK HAD EXPECTED his decision to be met with great joy. Instead, Sage looked like he had delivered the worst news possible.

Her soft lips took on the stubborn pout he knew so well.

"Except we're not a traditional family, any more than we're a traditional married couple."

Feeling as if his life was about to be blown to smithereens, he forced her to spell it out. "You don't want more?"

She paused, all cool elegance once again. "Of course I do."

Was this about the difference in the way they'd grown up? The fact that he'd never known the kind of luxury she had enjoyed before moving to Laramie, and might possibly want to savor again. Now that they had a baby to care for.

Sage inhaled sharply, abruptly looking as miserable deep down as he felt. "But…" She kept her eyes locked on his with effort. "We had a deal. Friends first. Lovers second. Co-parents third."

He remembered, and he regretted conceding what he had really wanted, in favor of expediency, and an alternate route to happiness.

"And then we became husband and wife," he reminded her.

She tensed, all the color leaving her face, then returning in a riotous bloom of color.

He didn't have to be a rocket scientist to see she was about to push him away again. "As was going to be required by your new business partners," she reminded him matter-of-factly.

Noting that Shane had fallen asleep again, she lifted him onto her shoulder and covered her breast with the edge of her hospital gown. "But we also agreed that wouldn't change anything between us. You would still have your goals and ambitions and I would have mine. We'd go our own ways and come together when we could."

Shane slept on.

Reining in the pain and disappointment he felt, Nick asked, "What are you trying to say?"

"That the mistake this morning was not yours, it was mine. I shouldn't have come on this trip with you at all. Not this close to my due date. Even if my OB gave me the go-ahead, with plenty of conditions, I should have realized the potential dangers and been a lot more cautious."

So this was it? She blamed herself for the chaos surrounding the medical emergency? "Come on, Sage. There was no way you could have known this would happen. You were a little over two weeks from your due date, and you weren't the least bit dilated when you saw the doctor yesterday."

"Actually," she admitted ruefully, "I think there might have been a sign or two."

He narrowed his eyes. "You told me that since the Braxton Hicks catastrophe you'd hardly felt even the slightest warm-up contraction."

"That's true. It was the lower back discomfort that kept getting to me, and last night, into this morning, it was pretty awful."

"Is that why you were so weepy and out of sorts when we were getting ready to go this morning?"

"In retrospect, I can see I was probably in labor all night. I just didn't think my inability to get comfortable was all that different from the usual, because as you well know, my back has bothered me the entire pregnancy."

He took a moment to reflect on that. "Well, I'm glad you went with me today. Because if you hadn't," he continued gruffly, "I might not have been there when you did give birth."

"So it all worked out. I got to be there to support you this morning, and witness the excitement of the grand opening of your new business venture. And you got to personally be the first to welcome little Shane into the world."

"But…?" he prodded, sensing there was more.

Sage sobered. "I still should have known better. And next time…if there is a next time…" Blushing, she stumbled over her words uncertainly, and for a moment, had to look away from him entirely.

She squared her slender shoulders determinedly. "And I don't mean having another child necessarily…but just the next time a choice like this has to be made." Once again, she met his gaze. "I'll make sure I do what's right for Shane first, and me second. And I'll step back and let you worry about you."

Her vow encompassed everything they had originally

promised each other. Yet it hit him like a sucker punch to the gut.

He took her free hand in his. "And that's good enough for you?" he asked, savoring the soft and silky warmth of her skin, the sweet womanly scent of her.

He moved onto the hospital bed so he could sit beside her. "You don't want more?" he asked quietly, as her thigh pressed intimately against his. "A traditional marriage and family? Or true, abiding love?" *The kind I could give you, if you'd only open up your heart and soul to the possibility?*

She stared down at their entwined fingers, thinking, deliberating. "Of course I do, theoretically," she responded in a low voice edged with resentment. "But realistically, Nick? I don't want you giving up anything for us that you're going to regret later, out of some misguided momentary notion of romantic love," she confided, her lower lip quavering.

Seeming on the verge of tears, she withdrew her hand from his and said, "I don't want you and me to make the same mistake that Terrence and I did, thinking we could rewrite the foundation of our relationship just through strength of will or because we thought that was what was expected of us. I don't want to risk everything we've had for something that might not pan out, that could ruin everything. For you, for me, for Shane. Especially now—" she inhaled a deep, shaky breath, looking protectively down at the baby cuddled against her "—when we're still caught up in the miracle of giving birth."

They were still in a daze over that, Nick thought, albeit—at least for him—a truly happy one.

Sage, on the other hand, seemed a lot more conflicted. Still, she had been through a lot in the last twenty-four hours, so he tried to rein in his hurt feelings and be patient.

Oblivious to his mounting frustration and dismay, she continued, "It's not surprising you'd want to give our son everything. Because I do, too. But we have to be level-headed and think about how this all began."

"Casually," he recollected, wishing like hell he'd told her the truth about his feelings in the beginning.

She nodded, accepting that. "With distinct, well-outlined limits."

Silence fell.

Nick thought about how much he had always hated being constrained—by anything. Especially rudimentary rules made long ago that had no bearing on what they were currently experiencing.

Treading carefully—he was dealing with a wife who had just given birth after all, a wife who might be experiencing a storm of mood-shifting hormones—he stifled his own soul-deep disappointment long enough to ask, very quietly, "What if that's not enough for me?"

For a moment, a defeat similar to what he felt flickered on her face. Then the fiercely independent Sage he'd first met returned. Her heart as guarded as ever. "If we want to make this all work long-term, if we want all our dreams to come true, it's going to have to be enough, Nick," she told him resolutely. "For both of us."

Chapter Sixteen

"For someone who just had a son, you're looking awfully blue," his older sister Erin said from the other side of the Triple Canyon ranch house kitchen. She set out glasses, ice and cold beverages for the Welcome to Our Two Families party for little Shane. Then paused to watch Nick set up the party-sized coffeemaker and hot water dispensers for tea and cocoa.

Her expression worried, she checked on the potluck casseroles warming in the oven. "And Sage doesn't look as happy as I would expect her to be, either."

Glad she was upstairs nursing the baby, and not privy to any of this—it was hard enough for him to hear it—Nick set out the platters of ham, brisket and chicken. "Shane was up most of both nights that they were in the hospital."

"You were there, too," Erin challenged. "Walking the floor with him."

Life was not as simple as his sisters sometimes thought. Nick swallowed. "Yes, I've lost sleep." *Over the mess our life is suddenly in.* "But Sage is the one who is nursing so I think it's harder on her."

Erin paused sympathetically. "What else is going on?"

Together, they set out the silverware and napkins. "I need to ask you something and I don't want you to get offended."

She grinned in amusement. "Well, that's a great start for a heart-to-heart."

"I'm serious." What he was about to broach was delicate, to say the least.

She sobered, too. Knowing they wouldn't have too much time before the rest of both clans started arriving, she touched his arm and encouraged softly, "Fire away. After all, what are big sisters for?"

Nick drew a breath, aware having one woman in the family disappointed in him was more than enough. He lounged against the counter, hands braced on either side of him. "Mac's made some jokes about the fact that when you had the twins, your hormones were way out of whack."

Erin laughed and rolled her eyes. "Ah…yeah. I cried at the drop of a hat."

Nick remembered.

Yet no one had seemed to think anything of it. It had all seemed so normal. What was happening between him and Sage wasn't. At least as far as he could figure, thus far. "Did that affect how you felt about things?"

Erin looked at him with perceptive eyes. "Like what, exactly?"

He swallowed around the tight knot in his throat. Pushed on resolutely. "Your marriage. Or what you wanted in the future or even the present."

"No. I know Mac is the one for me."

Pushing into more difficult territory, Nick presumed, "And that's different from your first marriage?"

"Yes. That was a mistake," Erin reflected candidly. "I mean, I can't regret it, because that union gave me Sammie and Stevie and Angelica, but I also know even if Angelica hadn't been diagnosed with leukemia, and our relationship hadn't been strained by her long illness and death, that our marriage never would have lasted."

Nick had been in middle school when they'd divorced. "How come?"

"We wanted different things. He needed his freedom. I needed someone I could count on to be there through thick and thin." Erin set out the appetizer trays. "Are you and Sage having problems?"

Nick shrugged. "I want things that she doesn't want." He'd thought time would fix it, allow them to finally get on the same page. But it hadn't. And now they seemed to have come full circle. To the strangers they had initially been to each other. With so much still out of reach. And he didn't know what in the hell to do about any of it. All he knew was that he didn't want to hurt Sage. Never had. Never would. And if that meant putting his own needs and desires on the back burner once again...

Erin's gaze narrowed speculatively. "Can you compromise?"

"I'm not sure," Nick admitted.

Abruptly, the sister who had raised him from age ten on looked as sad and concerned as he felt, deep down. "It's that serious?"

Reluctantly, Nick nodded.

Silence fell.

Finally, he said, "She still wants to raise Shane together and so do I."

"But not be married?" Erin guessed, her lips twisting in a troubled moue.

Nick went back to setting out the buffet. "We haven't spoken about divorce."

"But," Erin said, "you're worried that talk is coming."

Nick nodded stiffly.

Doing his best to pull it together, he said, "On the other

hand, the two of us have both been through a lot the past few days. Heck, make that the last five months. And as you've confirmed, her hormones are out of whack." Although his gut told him, not that out of whack...

"You want my advice?"

Not trusting himself to speak, he looked Erin in the eye.

"You've never been afraid to take risks in business. Or encourage me to do the same. It's why I spun off my boot-making business and moved with Mac to the Panhandle so he could continue taking Wind Energy to that part of the state, without having to be away from us all the time. Yes, I worried that all the change would be hard for us, but in the end our love for each other and our children saw us through."

And they were happy, Nick knew. Blissfully so. He forced the words out. "You're saying Sage and I have the same potential."

Erin clasped his shoulders. "If you take a good hard look at what's really going on with the two of you. And then take the kind of risks in your personal life that you're all too willing to take in business. Yeah, little brother, I really do."

"How much is Nick going to be traveling now?" Lucille asked as Sage finished nursing.

Sage handed Little One to her mother for burping. "I'm not sure." She walked into the adjacent bath to remove her robe and put on her party clothes.

Lucille paced, Shane on her shoulder. "You haven't discussed it?"

Sage slipped on a pair of white capris and walked out, still buttoning a sleeveless buttercup yellow blouse. Aware she needed her mother more than ever, she replied,

"Not recently. But initially, Nick wanted to take six weeks paternity leave, and then travel sporadically after that."

Her mom drew back and looked her in the eye. "And the venture capital company underwriting Upscale Outfitters?"

She wandered over to the mirror and frowned at the shadows beneath her eyes. "They want him back on the road by the end of the week." In Denver, no less!

"What do you want?"

Sage applied concealer beneath her eyes. Aware her mother was still awaiting an answer, she said, "I don't want to be the 'ball and chain' holding Nick back."

Lucille watched Sage put on foundation and blush. "Isn't there some compromise?"

"I wondered the same thing, but when I broached it on the way back from Dallas, Nick didn't want to talk about it." She frowned. "To me, anyway." After applying lipstick, then mascara, she spun back to her mom, who was in seventh heaven cuddling baby Shane.

"Has he talked to anyone?" Lucille asked.

Sage jerked in a breath. "He spent several hours yesterday afternoon at Metro Equity Partners office, meeting with MR and the team while Shane and I remained in the hospital, recuperating from the birth."

"And…?"

Sad and confused, she related how shut out she'd felt. Then and now. "Nick didn't want to talk about what was said then, either."

Her mother arched a brow in surprise.

"All I know for certain is that papers are being sent out this afternoon, for signature. Apparently, they couldn't get it all ready before he left Dallas."

Aware Shane had fallen fast asleep, her mother settled him in the beautiful wooden cradle that had been in Nick's family for generations.

Finished, Lucille straightened. "You think they gave him an ultimatum?"

Sage sat down to put on her shoes. "MR told me, in the hospital, he was going to have to be fully committed to being the spokesperson for Upscale Outfitters. Or else."

"That's why you did the local news interviews," Lucille ascertained.

While still in her hospital gown and robe, looking like heck. Sage forced herself not to grimace at the memory of being pressured by Nick's business associates. "The publicity was too good to pass up," she fibbed.

Her mom scowled. "Your father and I might have felt that way, in our heyday, but not you and Nick."

Sage edged closer, working to keep her voice low. "What are you saying?" she asked a great deal more casually than she felt.

"That maybe the real problem is, you're not being true to yourself. Or him, honey."

Tears pricked her eyes. "I don't want to pressure him," she admitted miserably. Which would certainly happen if she spilled everything. "He's been through enough recently, seeing the dream he had for expanding the legacy of Monroe's turn into something else entirely."

Lucille handed her a tissue. "I thought the grand opening of the new Dallas store went very well."

Sage dabbed the corners of her eyes. "In terms of sales, the reports were outstanding." Her throat clogged with suppressed emotion. "In terms of making Nick feel proud or triumphant?" she whispered hoarsely. "Not so much."

Lucille took Sage's arm and drew her over to sit side

by side on the bed. "So you're walking on eggshells around him."

"I want to support him, Mom, but not back him into a corner."

Lucille patted her hand. "The way the venture capital group is."

Sage nodded. "I'm afraid if I don't give him the room he needs to make all his professional dreams come true, he'll end up feeling trapped, and walk away from me, too." Just like Terrence had.

Her mother stood, thinking, and began to pace. "You're right," she said softly, turning back around. "It is a very tenuous situation. It won't, however, be the first and only crisis the two of you face as a married couple."

Sage looked at her mom uncomprehendingly.

"For everything that brings you and Nick together, there will be someone or something else just as powerful threatening to tear you apart."

Like MR and her partners. The relentless demands. The fact that I'm still afraid to tell Nick how I really feel.

Sage knotted her hands together on her lap. "If that's the case, what should I do?"

Lucille sat down beside her once again, and gently advised, "You have to have ask yourself, just how committed are you?"

More than he could ever—or maybe will ever—know, Sage thought.

"How much are you willing to let outside factors wedge distance between you and Nick?"

Not willing at all!

"Now for the most important question of all..." As usual, Lucille saved the biggest zinger for last. "Are you going to open up your heart—the way I've *yet* to see you do, honey—and *really* go after what you want?"

Which was Nick.

To be all hers.

All the time.

Sage thought about what her mom had said while she finished dressing for the party. She was just about to go downstairs and join the gathering of the Monroe and Lockhart clans, when she saw an unfamiliar sports car coming up the drive. It stopped behind the long rows of family vehicles. Everett emerged, thick yellow envelope in hand.

Realizing this was her opportunity to get started on her Rescue Our Marriage project, Sage slipped out the back and came around the side of the ranch house to intercept MR's assistant. Before she made a final decision on exactly how she was going to proceed next, there were a few things she had to know. She sensed he could help her.

She motioned the smartly dressed assistant over to where she was standing, out of view of the front windows. Brow arched curiously, he approached.

"I want to ask you something."

"Okay."

"That comment you made to me, the morning after Nick and I got married. When you told me that I hadn't gained a husband, and had instead lost my best friend." She searched his face. "What prompted you to say that?" What had MR's assistant known then, that she might still not?

A beat of silence fell. Finally, Everett held the envelope against his chest and allowed, "Look, I probably shouldn't have butted in that way. But I felt sorry for you."

Sage struggled to understand. "Because I had been ill?"

Grimacing, he corrected, "Because you were being played."

So maybe her intuition that MR wanted her out of the way had not been so off-kilter, after all. "In what way?"

"MR has a way of taking over people's realms without them ever knowing it. I'm a case in point. I haven't had a life since I started working for her."

"Then why continue?"

Everett let the package fall to his side. "She's going places. I want that kind of success, too. Being her sidekick is the fastest, surest way for me to climb the ladder myself."

Sage studied him closely.

"You really think MR's that single-minded?" In the hospital, although the venture capitalist had manipulated Sage to help her get what she and her partners wanted, she'd also seemed concerned about Nick's long-term happiness and future.

A terse nod. "Whatever she does is always for her own gain. If someone else benefits along the way, great." He shrugged. "If not, doesn't matter."

In retrospect, Sage could see that, too. "And I come in where…?"

For a moment, Everett seemed to battle with himself. Finally, he allowed, "You were the one thing standing in the way of Nick's triumph at Upscale Outfitters."

Were, Sage thought, focusing on the past tense of the statement. Not *are*… Her chest tightened. "So your boss was out to split us up from the get-go?"

He briefly inclined his head. "Let's just say she had her ways of making sure things did not go smoothly for the two of you, starting with the honeymoon."

"The shrimp that was ordered," Sage guessed.

Everett lifted a staying hand. "I don't know anything for sure. All I can assert is that she is the one who spoke to the hotel management. Every time."

Sage blinked. "But I thought the hotel took responsibility for the mistake."

"Of course they did."

Because the customer was always right, never more so than in a five-star hotel.

What Everett was intimating all made sense. And yet... "MR was the one who insisted Nick and I get married before he ever officially made a deal with Metro Equity Partners. Why do that," Sage continued curiously, "if she didn't want me around?"

"Because, as she said, a deadbeat dad would not have made a good spokesperson, and she didn't want a PR nightmare." Everett exhaled. "And because she also knew that the moment Nick had a ring on his finger, he would feel..."

"Trapped," Sage guessed.

He nodded. "Whereas if he hadn't made an honest woman of you, he would have felt guilty, and then been even more tied to you, trying to prove to everyone that he was a good guy."

"But, on the other hand, if he married me..." Sage said.

"Even briefly," Everett added.

"His being a good person would be assumed."

Everett continued, "Since he had done the honorable thing and had been responsible for you and the baby."

"MR told you all this?"

"She called it a teachable moment."

"So she wanted Nick for herself," she stated.

He exhaled. "She knew the two of you'd divorce if it eventually didn't work out due to Nick's heavy travel and work schedule."

Which MR had machinated every step of the way, Sage thought indignantly.

Everett continued with a poker face, "By then, of

course, Nick would be filthy rich as half owner of six luxury stores, and she could step in, reap the benefits. Go from being his boss/partner to boss/partner/wife."

Sage stared at him, amazed at the depth of the duplicity. "She said that, too?"

"Of course not, but I know how her mind works. I saw the way she pored over the publicity photos of Nick. I've seen her work with other clients. With Nick it was different." Everett paused to reflect. "But in the end, I guess I was really the one who was naive to think my giving you a heads-up would make a difference in the way things eventually worked out."

It had, and it hadn't, Sage thought, aware things weren't necessarily as "over" as Everett—and perhaps MR—thought. "Would you mind if I took the papers to Nick?" she asked, suddenly ready to do battle herself.

The door opened before Everett could reply and Nick stepped outside to join them.

"Not necessary. I'm here." He took the envelope from Everett. "Got a pen?"

Sage began to panic. Nick looked so determined. So grim. So ready to put it all behind him. Which was the last thing she wanted! "I really think you and I should talk," she said hurriedly.

Avoiding her eyes, Nick shook his head and said heavily, "Not about this, we don't."

SAGE STOOD WITH NICK, watching Everett drive away, hastily signed documents in hand. "Is Shane still doing okay?"

Nick nodded. "He's still sleeping but I brought him downstairs, so everyone can quietly admire him. Your mom said she'd text us if he wakes and needs to be fed, but in the meantime, how about you and I take a walk?"

"Sounds good," Sage said softly. She wanted the privacy. The chance to get everything back on the right track.

Although it wasn't clear from the implacable expression on Nick's face that this was what he wanted.

He led her down the gravel path to the pasture, where the ranch horses were grazing. "Those papers I just signed severed my relationship with Metro Equity Partners. I'm no longer a co-owner of, or the face of, Upscale Outfitters."

His news rocked her to the core. "That's a pretty big decision."

"And the right one." He rested his arms on the top of the wooden fence and gazed out at the land that had been in his family for generations. "I've known for some time it wasn't a good fit, either business-wise or personally." He flexed his broad shoulders resolutely. "I'm relieved to be out of it."

She could see that. And yet…there were other parts to his dreams. Ways he could be hurt. She moved closer still, inhaling the brisk masculine scent of his aftershave. "What about financially?"

He turned a level look her way. "Since I never put any of my own money into the start-up, most of what I lost was my time and effort." His sensual lips thinned ruefully. "But I can't complain given all I learned about what I don't want in a career path. I'm happy to be my own man again."

Sage could see that. She was happy for him, too. But scared that a change this huge in attitude and outlook could mean more in his personal life, too. Aware that the numbness she'd felt for the last several days was gone, the ache in her heart back full force, she forced herself to remain calm as she asked quietly, "Now what? Are you going to go back to just running Monroe's?" *Back to just being my friend, and lover, and nothing else...?*

Pivoting toward her, he rested an elbow on the top of the fence. He inclined his head, his emotional barriers still intact. "I still want more. But on my terms this time."

Unable to fault him for that, after all he'd been through, Sage hitched in a breath and told him sincerely, "I hope you get what you want."

"I'm sure I will in business." He flashed his most impersonal smile. "It's the rest of my life that's up in the air."

Hers, too.

His expression turned formidable. He looked her in the eye. "I don't want to travel anymore, Sage. I don't want to be away from you, and I don't want to be away from Shane."

Sage's pulse pounded. She felt on the verge of tears. "I don't want that, either," she admitted, aware it was now or never.

She took his hands in hers. Holding them tightly, she gazed up at him and admitted, "I never have."

Expression gentling, he pressed his forehead against hers. "Why didn't you say something?"

She hitched in an enervating breath. "Because I didn't want you to end up feeling robbed of anything, Nick. I didn't want you to feel trapped."

Lifting his head, Nick's gaze drifted over her, as if he were memorizing every detail. "The way you've been?"

The lump in her throat was back. Another wave of anxiety slid through her. Ignoring the sudden wobbliness of her knees, she tried to figure out where this was all going.

She knew if they ever had a prayer of making things work, she had to be completely honest with him. Tears blurred her vision. "I admit I regret marrying when and why we did."

The silence stretched between them, emphasizing all that was at stake. His jaw clenched. "So do I."

Calling on every ounce of courage she had, Sage pushed on. "I regret the way we started our family, too." She studied their entwined hands, then looked deep into his eyes, admitting tremulously, "I wish we had done it out of love, not practicality."

He squinted.

"Are you talking about your feelings now—or mine?" he demanded gruffly.

Here was her chance. To open up her heart. Go for broke. "Yours. But it's okay," she rushed on, as he wrapped an arm about her waist, and would have drawn away, but held fast. She splayed her hands over his chest. "You don't have to view our relationship romantically."

"I don't?" he echoed in shock.

"No," she said. "Because I have enough in my heart for both of us."

"Except I do feel that way about you, Sage. I have from the very first. I just didn't tell you how I really felt because I knew you weren't in a place where you could take a risk like that."

"So you opted to be my friend instead."

"And then lover. And then father of our hoped-for child," he recollected rustily, wiping away her tears with the tip of his fingertip. "The night we married was one of the happiest times of my life."

"Mine, too. At least," Sage amended ruefully, "until we got to the hotel."

"And MR had a surprise waiting for us."

She paused in shock, asked warily, "You know about that?"

He nodded curtly, his disillusionment and disappointment as sharp as her own. "I talked to The Mansion hotel manager the evening before the grand opening. He felt terrible about what had happened before, about the fact that the order was written up to specifically request shrimp, instead of exclude it. He assumed it was a data entry error from the room service department."

"But you knew better?"

"I had been there when MR pulled a similar stunt with one of the suppliers, blamed it on one of their younger sales reps and then used the mix-up to leverage a lower margin on their goods. So I figured it was her."

"Did you confront her?" she asked.

He nodded. "It was what we were talking about, in the office, when we got to the store that morning."

"Right before I interrupted."

"And then later, at the MEP office the next day. MR said she was only helping me out. Speeding the process of me discovering you were all wrong for me." Anger simmered in his eyes. "The ironic thing is that I had already realized that I could not continue to be in partnership with someone that manipulative and deceitful."

He paused, grimacing, and her heart went out to him.

Soberly, he continued, "I knew I had to go through with the grand opening, and make sure I did my part in publicly launching the new venture. I owed the other partners that. But I planned to tell you I was going to end things as soon as I could."

"Only I went into labor before any of that could happen…" Sage recollected.

"And little Shane was born." He paused, sharing the happy memory of their son's tumultuous but ultimately victorious entrance into the world, via his daddy's help.

Sobering, Nick went back to the reasons behind his

decision. "The worst thing is I had a sixth sense that MR was trying to undermine the two of us all along."

"Apparently, Everett thought so, too." Sage went on to reveal the gist of her conversation with MR's assistant the morning after the wedding. "Unfortunately, instead of trying to avoid that pitfall and talk to you about what he'd said to me, and the need for us to keep the lines of communication open and make our friendship—which is the foundation of our entire relationship—even stronger, I let the seeds of doubt grow. Jeopardizing our potential to stay close and happy, at every turn."

Nick reflected soberly, his gaze as sincere as it was tender. "Seems like we should have done a lot more talking."

Sage nodded. "About what was really in our hearts and on our minds." She wreathed her arms about his neck and stood on tiptoe. Her heart brimmed with happiness. "Because I'm crazy in love with you, Nick. I want to be all in, all the time, from here on out." She kissed him.

He pulled her close and kissed her back, passionately and evocatively. Until her toes curled and her knees threatened to buckle. "I'm crazy in love with you, too," he admitted thickly.

Their gazes locked as readily as their smiles. At last, it seemed, they were as committed to their relationship and each other as she had always wanted to be.

"So," she prodded softly, "what do you say we make ours a real marriage, in every way?"

Nick grinned broadly. "Sweetheart, I'm all in. And one more thing…" He reached into his pocket and withdrew a velvet jeweler's box. "I haven't yet given you your push present."

Sage lifted the lid. Inside was a stunning diamond solitaire. "Oh, Nick…" she breathed.

Epilogue

"It's amazing, what a difference the right business plan can make," Sage murmured two years later, as she and Nick took one last look around the satellite store, before calling it a night.

The first Monroe's Outpost was set to open the following morning. Located on Main Street, in the county seat of a rural county just west of Laramie, the brand-new mercantile bore the same distinctive Texas atmosphere as the original Monroe's Western Wear.

Although much smaller in scope, it was well-designed and well-outfitted with every necessary item a cowgirl or cowboy could need. The boots, jeans, shirts, chaps, jackets, hats and belts were both high-quality and reasonably priced.

Nick looked around with a pride she and his family all shared. "I think Mom and Dad would be proud to know we were bringing a needed service to this community."

Sage nodded happily. "And the other rural community stores that will come in the next decade."

All without requiring any outside capital, or interference.

The clatter of little cowboy boots sounded on the wood floor. Sage followed Shane as he raced curiously down the aisle. "Trust me," she teased, over her shoulder, "if there is one thing every busy parent knows, the less time it takes to get any task accomplished, the better."

In her life, and many others, convenience was key.

"And that's only going to be truer five months from now," she said, as Nick caught up with them.

"I imagine that's so," Nick predicted, tenderly wrapping one arm around her shoulders. "Although—" he curved a hand lovingly over her blossoming tummy "—Shane doesn't seem to mind going places now."

Sage leaned against her husband's chest. She rested her head on his shoulder, as their little boy took his pint-sized hat off his head, let out a whoop worthy of a rodeo cowboy and tossed it in the air. He hooted again as it clattered to the floor. "Because we're letting him run around and explore, unfettered. The minute we strap him into his car seat…"

Nick chuckled. "He'll let us know he would much rather be free."

Sage grinned as Shane caught sight of himself in the mirror, then resettled his hat and paused to reflect.

She turned back to Nick, splaying her hands against the solid warmth of his chest. "Think he comes by his independent spirit naturally?"

"Probably." Nick kissed Sage's temple and smoothed a hand through her hair. "But he also has a boundless ability to love."

They all did, Sage thought contentedly.

Shane stopped just short of them. He lifted his hands, signaling his desire to be picked up.

Nick obliged.

Shane smiled happily, then leaned over and put his hand on Sage's tummy, as he had seen his daddy do. "Baby. In there," he declared.

Nick and Sage smiled. "There sure is, little dude," Nick said proudly.

Shane's smile broadened. "I like babies."

Her heart overflowing with gratitude and joy, Sage bussed the top of her little boy's head. "We all do."

Shane grabbed a fistful of each of their shirtfronts and pulled them in for a group hug. "I love Mommy and Daddy, too," he said adamantly.

"We love you, too," Nick and Sage said in unison.

Shane squinted comically. They squinted mischievously back. Then they all began to laugh. Life, Sage thought, did not get any better than this.

* * * * *

Watch for the final story in Cathy Gillen Thacker's
TEXAS LEGACIES: THE LOCKHARTS *miniseries,*
A TEXAS SOLDIER'S CHRISTMAS.
Coming November 2017,
only from Harlequin Western Romance!

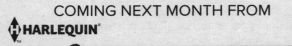

Get 2 Free Books,

HARLEQUIN® *Western Romance*

Plus 2 Free Gifts—
just for trying the
Reader Service!

SPECIAL EXCERPT FROM

H HARLEQUIN

ᴥWestern ᴥRomance

*Of all the towns in Texas Poppy White could
have chosen, she settled on Stonewall Crossing—the
town where Toben Boone, rodeo cowboy and father
to her son, lives…*

*Read on for a sneak preview of
A SON FOR THE COWBOY,
part of* **THE BOONES OF TEXAS**
miniseries by Sasha Summers.

Toben carried the large white box with breakfast treats back around the corner. He knocked on the shop door, smiling at the boy who opened it.

"Can I help you?" the boy asked, all brash confidence, boots and a shiny belt buckle.

"Got a breakfast delivery from Pop's Bakery. Welcome to the neighborhood." He held the box out.

"Thanks, mister. That's real nice."

"You a cowboy?" an older, sullen boy asked.

"I'd like to think so," Toben answered.

"If you're a cowboy, where's your horse?" the girl asked, hands on her hips. "Don't real cowboys ride horses?"

"Sometimes they drive a truck, like your aunt. She's a real cowgirl."

"She's the best," the smaller boy said, smiling at Poppy. "Four-time national champion. Third-fastest barrel racing time ever. Onetime international champion—"

"Oh my gosh, Rowdy, do we have to hear it again?" the girl asked. "We get it. She's awesome."

The younger boy glared at the other two. "You don't get it. Or you'd think it's awesome, too."

Poppy placed her hand on the younger boy's shoulder. "Thanks for bringing food. I'm hoping once they're fed, they'll be a little more civilized."

"I can't wait for them to go home." Rowdy sighed after the other two had left the room.

"You get to stay longer?" Toben asked.

"Nah, we live here now."

Wait, was Poppy a mom?

"Better hurry before they eat it all," Poppy said.

The boy ran from the room, and Poppy sighed. "Listen, Toben, he hasn't figured out who you are. I mean, he knows your name—but…" She shook her head. "Just let me tell him you are…you. Okay?"

Toben stared at her. "You lost me."

"Rowdy knows Toben Boone is his father. But you didn't introduce yourself so he doesn't know you are Toben Boone."

Toben felt numb all over. "Rowdy?"

"That was Rowdy," she repeated.

"I don't know what you're talking about, Poppy. But if you're trying to tell me I'm a…father…" He sucked in a deep breath, his chest hurting so much he pressed a hand over his heart. "Don't you think you waited a little long to tell me I have a son?"

Don't miss A SON FOR THE COWBOY by Sasha Summers, available July 2017 wherever Harlequin® Western Romance books and ebooks are sold.

www.Harlequin.com